Chasing the Dream

There in the water, poking its head right up to look back at them, was a dolphin. It had the coloring of a bottle-nosed dolphin; the back and head a uniform steely gray. . . .

"Oh, Frida, *querida!*" Luisa exclaimed. She had been wearing a swimsuit with a sarong wrapped and tied into a sort of dress. Now, with a quick movement, she pulled the sarong off, kicked off her rubber-soled sandals, then leaped over the side of the boat into the water to join her friend.

Look out for more titles in this series

Dolphin Diaries ™

Ben M. Baglio

Illustrations by Judith Lawton

CHASING THE DREAM

AN
APPLE
PAPERBACK

SCHOLASTIC INC.
New York Toronto London Auckland Sydney
Mexico City New Delhi Hong Kong Buenos Aires

No part of this publication may be reproduced in whole or in part, or stored in a retrieval system, or transmitted in any form or by any means, electronic, mechanical, photocopying, recording, or otherwise, without written permission of the publisher. For information regarding permission, write to Working Partners Limited, 1 Albion Place, London W6 0QT, United Kingdom.

ISBN 0-439-31951-X

Text copyright © 2001 by Working Partners Limited.
Illustrations copyright © 2001 by Judith Lawton.

All rights reserved. Published by Scholastic Inc., 555 Broadway, New York, NY 10012, by arrangement with Working Partners Limited. DOLPHIN DIARIES is a trademark of Working Partners Limited. SCHOLASTIC, APPLE PAPERBACKS, and associated logos are trademarks and/or registered trademarks of Scholastic Inc.

12 11 10 9 8 7 6 5 4   2 3 4 5 6 7/01

Printed in the U.S.A.   40
First Scholastic printing, February 2002

Special thanks to Lisa Tuttle

**Thanks also to the Whale and Dolphin
Conservation Society for reviewing the
information contained in this book**

1

September 14 — afternoon — Dolphin Haven.

I'm sitting by the side of the nursery pool, feeling a little sad because I have to say good-bye to Misty and Merlin, Evie and Dawn, Bella and Lola. I wish I could stay and see the calves grow up! Alicia and Dan have promised to send lots of pictures and keep us up-to-date, but I am really going to miss them. Seeing Merlin and Dawn born was such an amazing experience, I'll always feel close to them . . .

Jody McGrath stopped writing in her diary, and looked out at the water. The nursery pool here at

Dolphin Haven in the Bahamas was an area that had been fenced off from the large, natural lagoon that was the dolphins' usual home. The new mothers — all bottle-nosed dolphins — felt safer in this more protected environment, and it was easier for the staff at Dolphin Haven to keep an eye on the newborns.

For the past four weeks, the McGrath family and the crew of their boat, *Dolphin Dreamer*, had been helping out, sharing in the excitement of the dolphin births. But now it was time to move on.

Jody's parents, Craig and Gina McGrath, were marine biologists. Their latest research project, Dolphin Universe, was taking the McGraths all over the world to study dolphins. Sometimes Jody couldn't believe how lucky she was!

Misty swam past with her calf, Merlin, so close to her side that he looked glued on! He surfaced for air at the same time as his mother, but his flopping and splashing were very different from her graceful motion. He still had a lot to learn, Jody thought, smiling at his efforts.

Evie and her calf, Dawn, were not far away. The big dolphin lay quietly in the water while Dawn suckled.

Meanwhile, Bella and Lola were keeping watch, swimming slowly around the pair to make sure they were undisturbed. In the wild, Jody knew, mother dolphins relied on help from other adult females, referred to as "aunts." They kept away predators, and took on baby-sitting duties to give the mother a chance to hunt or rest. Even though they were all perfectly safe here at Dolphin Haven, Bella and her grown-up daughter took their jobs seriously.

"You're really going to miss those guys, aren't you?" Her father's voice took Jody by surprise. She looked around, startled, and found her parents smiling down at her.

She got to her feet. "It's hard to say good-bye to them," she said wistfully.

"I know, sweetheart." Her mother gave her a brief hug. "But think about all the other dolphins we're going to meet after we leave here!"

Jody brightened and grinned back at her mom, starting to get excited. It was impossible to resist her enthusiasm!

Just then, they heard Alicia Levy, one of the managers of Dolphin Haven, calling to them.

3

It's hard to say good–bye . . .

Looking around, Jody saw Alicia approaching with a young woman she had never seen before.

"Craig, Gina, Jody . . ." Alicia began. "This is Luisa Suarez of the Whale and Dolphin Protection League." Then she turned to the visitor. "Luisa, I'd like you to meet Doctors Craig and Gina McGrath, and their daughter, Jody, from Dolphin Universe."

Luisa Suarez, a slender young woman whose glossy

black hair was neatly bobbed, gave a small gasp. "Dolphin Universe! *¡Ay mí!* I know of it — you have a wonderful website!" She had a dazzling smile.

Gina grinned back at her. "Thank you!"

Jody wondered why neither Alicia nor Dan had mentioned they were expecting visitors today.

"Is this an official visit?" Craig asked, clearly thinking the same thing.

"Semi-official," Luisa replied, smiling. "It was a spur-of-the-moment thing, really, because Dolphin Haven isn't actually due for an inspection. But I happened to be in Nassau at a conference when I heard that some dolphin calves had just been born . . ." She held up her hands. "I confess," she said jokingly. "I'm a sucker for baby animals, and I've never seen newborn dolphin calves. I thought there would be no harm in visiting to check on their condition."

She turned to Alicia and continued, "But since Dolphin Haven has such a good reputation, I'm confident that there won't be any problems." Then her smile faded. "I wish that was the case everywhere," she added.

"Well, we won't hold up your inspection tour," Craig

said with a friendly smile. "It was nice meeting you, but we have to be on our way."

Luisa looked disappointed. "Oh, do you have to go right away? I'd love to talk to you more about Dolphin Universe!"

Jody's parents exchanged a glance.

Then Craig nodded. "I think we could manage to stick around a little bit longer," he said. "It would be useful for us to get an update on your organization's work, too. How about if we go up to the kitchen, get a pot of coffee started, and you can join us up there for a chat after your inspection?"

"That sounds great!" Luisa replied as Alicia smiled and nodded.

"See you later, then," said Gina, as she and Craig began to move away. "Jody?"

Jody hesitated, reluctant to leave the dolphins.

Alicia noticed, and smiled at her. "Why don't you come with us?" she suggested.

"Thanks!" Jody beamed happily.

Luisa took photos of the dolphins in the nursery

pool. "Do you let visitors get into the water with the dolphins?" she asked.

"Not with these dolphins," Alicia said firmly. "We allow 'close encounters' with some of our dolphins, under strict supervision. But the calves need special care. We won't take any risks with their health. In a few more weeks, if they continue to thrive, we'll allow visitors . . . but they'll only be allowed to watch the dolphins in the nursery pool, not to handle them."

Finally, Luisa turned to Alicia and said she was satisfied that the dolphins were well cared for. "My dream is a world where no dolphins or whales are kept in captivity," she added. "But until my dream comes true, I am relieved to see captive dolphins treated as well as this."

Alicia nodded. "Thank you," she replied. "Dolphins aren't just a business to us, you know . . . they're our life. Dan and I are as devoted to our dolphins as if they were our children."

"Yes, I see that," Luisa said softly. Then she smiled. "Did someone say something about coffee?"

*   *   *

Dan Levy, Alicia's husband, was in their big, sunny kitchen with Craig and Gina.

"You're just in time," he said, putting a plate of blueberry muffins on the table.

"Just in time to stop you from eating all of those?" Alicia teased. She introduced him to Luisa and explained what they'd been doing.

Jody slid into a seat beside her mother and reached for a muffin.

"That coffee smells wonderful," Luisa said, inhaling deeply.

"I'll give you an extra-big mug, then," said Dan, going to the coffeepot. "Craig and Gina were telling me you've just been to a conference in Nassau — is that something we should have known about?"

Luisa shook her head. "Not unless you're involved in the international airfreight industry," she told him, smiling.

"We weren't the last time I looked," Dan replied jokingly. He looked puzzled. "I thought it must be something to do with dolphins. So why were *you* there?"

"To advise on the proper treatment of animals being

carried by air," Luisa explained. "That can include everything from pets to livestock to wild animals, including dolphins. There's been trouble recently with dolphins suffering through bad transportation. It was a last-minute decision that I should attend and speak about this."

"You seem to specialize in last-minute decisions," Alicia said, smiling.

Luisa made a wry face. "Yes . . . and now I may have to pay by spending a very long time at the airport, waiting for a cheap standby seat back to Kingston!"

"Kingston," Craig repeated. "So home is Jamaica?"

Luisa nodded. "Sort of," she replied. "I'm Mexican. My real home is Mexico City. But I patrol the area between Cuba, Haiti, and Jamaica. My boat — that is, the League's boat — is anchored off the northwest coast of Jamaica, and I guess that the boat is home for now."

"You know," Craig said thoughtfully. "The next leg of our journey will take us down through the Windward Passage, and right by Jamaica."

Gina nodded in agreement. "Of course, it will take at least three or four days to get there, so if you're in a big hurry, you might consider flying. But you're welcome to come with us," she said with a warm smile at Luisa.

"And we could take you right to your boat," Craig added.

Luisa stared open-mouthed at the McGraths. "You'd do that for me? For nothing? When you don't even know me?" she gasped in astonishment.

"My parents can be a bit impulsive, too, sometimes," Jody told her, grinning.

Gina laughed. "Not at all!" she protested, shaking her head at Jody. Turning back to Luisa, she explained, "Even though we've only just met you, Luisa, we're very familiar with the good work done by the Whale and Dolphin Protection League."

"And we'd like to learn more," Craig added. "So far, Dolphin Universe hasn't had as much input from conservation groups as we'd like."

"So, you see, you'd be doing *us* a favor, too," Gina said. "While we're sailing, you can fill us in on the work you're doing and make a contribution to Dolphin Universe!"

"I could talk your ear off if you let me," Luisa said warningly. "Do you know what you're getting into?"

"No," Craig admitted with a grin. "But I hope we're going to find out."

"It's a deal!" Her warm brown eyes sparkling, Luisa set down her empty mug on the table and stood up. "When do we sail?"

An hour later, Jody and her parents and Luisa arrived at the slip where *Dolphin Dreamer* was berthed. During the ten-minute walk between Dolphin Haven and the island marina, Luisa had kept them all entertained with stories about her adventures working for the Whale and Dolphin Protection League — or WDPL as it was called for short. Jody felt sure that the next few days with Luisa on board would be interesting.

Sean and Jimmy, Jody's eight-year-old twin brothers, were playing on deck and came charging forward as they boarded.

"Hey, Dad, Harry says —" Jimmy stopped short as he caught sight of Luisa. "Who's *that?*" he demanded.

"This is Luisa Suarez," Mr. McGrath replied.

"Luisa, these are my sons, Sean and Jimmy," Gina added. To the boys, she explained, "We're giving Luisa a lift back to her own boat."

Jimmy looked thoughtful. "Okay, that's cool," he decided. His twin nodded agreement.

"Where's Harry?" Craig asked.

"Everybody else is down below," Jimmy explained. "We're keeping a lookout in case there are pirates or anybody wanting to cause trouble."

"Keep up the good work," Craig said solemnly before leading the others below deck.

In the main cabin, Maddie was working on a laptop computer. She looked up as they entered.

"Maddie, this is Luisa Suarez," Gina began. "Luisa, please meet our invaluable assistant, Maddie."

"Pleased to meet you," Luisa said, thrusting out her hand.

Maddie rose and shook it. "*Con mucho gusto*," she replied politely in Spanish.

Luisa smiled delightedly and responded with a flood of Spanish. It was too fast for Jody, who, so far, had only taken one year of Spanish at school. But Maddie obviously had no problem, and they spoke together for a minute.

Finally Luisa stopped, looking guilty. "I'm sorry — we should stick to English, so everyone can understand! I got carried away — it's so nice to hear my own language again."

"Your English is wonderful," Gina told her. "Craig and I picked up a little Spanish during our graduate studies, but it's pretty rusty."

"And I've just started learning it," Jody added.

"Maybe having Luisa on board will encourage you to work harder," Maddie said with a mock frown. She told Luisa, "The other part of my job is teaching Jody, Brittany, Sean, and Jimmy while they're away from their regular schools."

"Who is Brittany?" Luisa asked, turning to Jody. "Is she your sister?"

Jody quickly shook her head. "No, she's Harry's daughter — Harry's our captain."

"Is somebody talking about me?" The familiar, deep voice made them all look around. Harry Pierce came

13

in, a smile on his bearded, weather-beaten face. His second mate, Cameron Tucker, a fit, handsome young man, was right behind him.

Craig introduced them both to Luisa and explained the situation.

Harry nodded thoughtfully. "That's fine. Jamaica's right on the route I had planned to take to the Lesser Antilles. So let's get going!"

2

Jody found Brittany in their cabin, sprawled across her bunk with the laptop computer they shared for schoolwork.

"Could I use the computer for a few minutes, please, Brittany?" Jody asked.

Brittany scowled, staring at the screen. "Can't you see I'm busy?"

"Only for a minute. I just want to check my e-mail before we set sail," Jody explained.

The other girl shook her head impatiently. "Not now. Maddie told me to do this."

Jody bit her lip with frustration. "Please, Brittany. I need to go online before we set sail," she said. "The land-line will be disconnected in a few minutes!"

"Well, you'll just have to wait till I'm done," Brittany snapped.

It was too much. Jody frowned. "Look, that was supposed to be *my* computer, you know —"

"Yes, I do know!" Brittany sat up and glared at her. "Thanks for reminding me! Your computer, your cabin, everything here is *yours!*" Her gray eyes glistened with self-pity.

"That's not true," Jody said unhappily. Brittany was a pain, but she did feel sorry for her. For Jody, being a part of her parents' research project was a dream come true, but Brittany had no interest in dolphins. She'd been forced to go with her father, the boat's captain, when her mother had decided to go on her own to visit her fiancé in France. "We just have to share, that's all," Jody told her firmly.

"Well, I hate sharing," Brittany complained. "At home I had my own computer and my own room and —"

"Me, too," Jody said hotly.

Their eyes met. Brittany looked startled, as if it had never occurred to her that anyone besides herself could have reason to complain.

She gave in suddenly, pushing the laptop so that the screen faced Jody. "Go on, then," she said, in a bored voice. "I'm fed up with homework anyway."

Jody was pleased to discover not only a long e-mail from her best friend, Lindsay, but also the weekly newsletter from her school back home in Florida. She saved them both to read later, then turned to Brittany. "Why don't you check your e-mail?" she suggested. "We're still online."

Brittany shrugged, as if she didn't care, but she pulled the computer back toward her and clicked the mouse. Her face suddenly lit up. "Hey, there's a letter from my mom!" she exclaimed happily.

Jody smiled, and she slipped away, leaving Brittany to read it on her own.

That evening, for the first time in weeks, dinner was served while *Dolphin Dreamer* traveled steadily across the waves of the open sea.

Everyone except Cam and Harry, who would eat later when someone else was on watch, gathered around the big table in the main cabin. The wind was strong but steady and their progress was smooth. But after more than three weeks on land, Jody found the constant motion of the boat a little strange. Harry had warned it might take a few days for them all to find their "sea legs" again.

Dr. Jefferson Taylor picked his way cautiously across the shifting floor to the table. He gave a gasp of surprise at the sight of Luisa Suarez. "My goodness, who is this?" He looked around the table in bewilderment. Jody thought he looked relieved to find that all the other faces were familiar ones.

Gina came to the rescue. "I'm sorry, Dr. Taylor, I forgot you hadn't been introduced yet. This is Luisa Suarez, who works for the Whale and Dolphin Protection League. We're giving her a lift back to her boat. While she's with us she'll be able to tell us some things about the work her organization is doing, which could contribute a lot to our project." She smiled at Luisa and went on, "Luisa, this is our colleague, Dr. Jefferson Taylor. He's employed by PetroCo, the company that sponsors Dolphin Universe."

"Glad to meet you, Dr. Taylor," Luisa said. She cocked her head curiously. "What exactly is your role on board *Dolphin Dreamer*?"

Dr. Taylor looked a little uncomfortable as he tried to answer her question. "Er, well, you see . . . my being here as PetroCo's representative shows the world that PetroCo is taking an . . . *active* . . . interest in our environment . . ." He frowned uneasily, then brightened as he thought of something else. "Plus, of course, I also have a lot of valuable scientific experience to offer!" he added.

"I'm sure you must be a great help," Luisa murmured politely.

Jody bit her lip, trying not to grin. In her opinion, Dr. Taylor was completely useless, but a major condition of PetroCo's sponsorship had been that one of their employees must be included as part of the crew on board *Dolphin Dreamer.*

Mei Lin set a tureen of a fragrant shrimp curry on the table beside a big bowl of rice. "Please, everybody help yourself," she urged, as she took her own seat. Mei Lin was not only the cook, but also the boat's engineer — Harry, who had hired her, declared she was a genius mechanic. Jody didn't know anything about engine mechanics, but she thought the young Chinese woman was a wonderful cook.

Dr. Taylor certainly agreed. His eyes brightened as soon as the food appeared, and he sniffed the air appreciatively. "You're in for a real treat here," he told Luisa happily, rubbing his hands. "May I serve you?"

September 16 — just after breakfast — Atlantic Ocean
  <u>*Spinner Dolphins*</u> *(Stenella longirostris)*
I'm so excited! A group of at least fifty spinner dolphins has been racing along beside us for the last ten minutes, leaping out and twirling in the air. It's the first time I've seen this species, and they are gorgeous! They are tri-colored: dark gray backs, light gray sides, and pale, pinkish-white bellies. They have longer, thinner snouts than either the bottle-nosed or spotted dolphins, but are otherwise similar in shape and size.

There's no wonder about how they got their name: the

They're not called spinners for nothing!

most amazing thing about them is the way they spin. I thought that the bottle-nosed dolphins were great acrobats, but I've never seen anything like this! They are really fast, too. They positively shoot up out of the water, and then twirl their bodies around and around in the air — like ballerinas gone wild. I watched one really carefully and it did seven complete spins — I counted! — before falling back into the water.

Jody paused to gaze out at the glistening bodies of the spinner dolphins as they leaped and plunged alongside *Dolphin Dreamer.* She felt the salt spray on her face, and was careful to shield her diary from the flying droplets of water.

Gina was standing at the railing nearby with the camcorder, recording the beautiful display. Nearby, Craig, Maddie, Luisa, Mei Lin, and the twins were all watching the amazing sight with wonder. Only Brittany and Dr. Taylor weren't on deck.

Brittany had shrugged and looked bored when Cam had shouted down to announce the arrival of the spinner dolphins. She was in another one of her moods.

Dr. Taylor had come up to watch for a few minutes but then went below again, tempted by the last two flaky croissants on the table.

Jody wished she could sketch the dolphins, but she was afraid it would be a wasted effort. The most amazing thing about them was their movement, and she knew she couldn't capture that in a still picture. She stood up and leaned against the side, watching longingly as the large group began to move away from the boat.

As they began to disappear into the distance, Jody sat down and wrote some more:

Dad said that spinner dolphins can dive much deeper than the Atlantic spotted dolphins, and travel in even bigger groups. He's seen groups of hundreds traveling together — maybe even as many as a thousand in one big, friendly group! There used to be lots more spinner dolphins than there are now. Hundreds of thousands of spinner dolphins were killed by the tuna-fishing industry during the 1970s and 1980s. Luisa said that, although some dolphins still get killed, things are much better to-

day, because conservation campaigns have brought about laws to help protect the dolphins. But the spinner dolphin population may never totally recover from so many deaths.

"Hi, Jody — what are you writing?"

Luisa's voice startled Jody out of her sad thoughts. She looked up. "I'm keeping a dolphin diary," she explained.

"What a great idea!" Luisa said enthusiastically.

"How did you first get interested in dolphins?" Jody asked curiously.

"I was younger than you are now," Luisa replied. "I was nine or ten years old when my parents took me to a dolphin show. I guess you could say it was love at first sight."

She came and sat down next to Jody, then went on. "I thought I was so lucky to be able to meet such wonderful creatures, to get up close to them, pet them, and even feed them fish. I thought that they jumped through hoops and did somersaults in the air because they were happy. I didn't know then that the owners of the show would starve them unless they performed."

Jody shook her head, horrified.

"It's true, I'm afraid," Luisa said quietly. "Not all people look after dolphins as well as Alicia and Dan." She sighed, then continued. "I began to read about dolphins. And soon I questioned whether these creatures, who were born to have the freedom of the seas, could be happy cooped up in the tiny, concrete tanks I'd seen them kept in. My mother said of course the dolphins were happy — they were smiling!"

Luisa's own smile was sad. "I was only a child, but even then I could see that the 'smile' was just the shape of the dolphin mouth. It looks like a smile to us, but dolphins can't frown, or look any other way. It doesn't mean they are happy. The next time my parents took me to see the show, I noticed that one of the dolphins didn't look well. She just lay still in the water, ignoring everything. Someone poked her with a stick, and still she had her dolphin 'smile' . . ." Luisa paused. "I learned a few days later that the dolphin had died," she finished.

Jody caught her breath in horror. "Do you know why?" she asked.

"I think she didn't want to live like that," Luisa told her. She gestured out at the water, where the spinner dolphins were playing in the distance. "They are beautiful, aren't they? People like to watch them. So, some people see they can make money if they catch them and put them on display. Spinner dolphins were some of the first dolphins to be captured for aquariums. But they don't survive well in captivity. It is even harder for them than for the bottle-nosed. Spinner dolphins need deep, deep water to dive, and wide, wide spaces to race and leap and spin. Without their freedom, they die."

Jody frowned, struggling with this idea. "The dolphins at Dolphin Haven didn't seem unhappy," she began.

"Dolphin Haven isn't the usual sort of dolphin display," Luisa reminded her. "It's a controlled habitat, more like a park than a zoo. Their dolphins stay in the ocean, not in tanks, and Alicia and Dan are both trained vets, who care very much about the health and happiness of their dolphins. People and places like that aren't the real problem." She paused and looked deep into Jody's eyes. "I hope you never have to see the sort of place that *is* the problem," she said seriously.

Just then, Maddie came out on deck. "Jody," she called. "It's time for school!"

Luisa looked around at Maddie. "Would you like some help?" she offered.

"That would be great!" Maddie replied, her eyes sparkling. "Why don't you take the girls for Spanish, then I can give the boys my undivided attention for math."

Sean and Jimmy groaned dramatically.

Jody knew how they felt. Her own heart sank. Spanish was her worst subject — and one of Brittany's best — as Brittany never failed to remind her.

Luisa must have noticed the sudden change in Jody's expression. She gave a puzzled-sounding laugh and patted her on the back. "Hey, don't worry, *chica*," she said. "I promise, no hard tests! No tests at all — I don't like them. We're just going to chat, like we were just now, only in Spanish instead of in English. It will be fun, not like work at all!" she finished persuasively.

Jody couldn't help smiling back. She just hoped

Luisa was right! She followed Luisa to join Brittany at the table in the main cabin.

At first, Jody had no trouble in understanding what Luisa said. In her role as a teacher, Luisa was careful to speak clearly and in simple sentences. It helped that she used her hands a lot, and her face was very expressive. Jody managed to follow Luisa's description of how she lived by herself on a small boat — much smaller than this one — and kept watch on the dolphins in the area between Jamaica, Cuba, and Haiti.

But when Luisa started talking about someone called Frida, Jody lost track a little. "Who's Frida?" she asked.

"*En español, por favor*," Luisa reminded her.

Jody bit her lip and tried again. "*¿Quien es Frida?*"

Luisa smiled, rather mysteriously, Jody thought. In Spanish, she replied that Frida was her friend, and very special. She added that she was looking forward to introducing Frida to all her new friends on *Dolphin Dreamer.*

Jody was still puzzled. She was sure that Luisa had said she lived by herself on her boat and that she stayed out at sea most of the time. So when did she manage to see her friend Frida, and how would they be able to meet her? Raising her hand again, Jody struggled to put her questions into Spanish.

But it must have come out wrong, because Brittany gave a loud, contemptuous snort.

Jody froze, humiliated.

Luisa looked sympathetic. She said something in Spanish which seemed to be a suggestion to try again.

But Jody's mind had gone blank. She couldn't recall a single word in Spanish. She could only shake her head and stare miserably down at the tabletop.

After a moment, Luisa said something to Brittany.

The other girl answered as smoothly as if she'd been practicing for weeks. She and Luisa traded questions and answers for a few minutes while Jody sat there, struggling to get over her embarrassment and follow along.

When Luisa next invited a comment from her, Jody managed a reply. But she knew immediately that she'd gotten something wrong when Brittany snorted rudely again.

Gently, Luisa corrected Jody's pronunciation of a couple of words, then praised her heartily when she repeated them correctly.

At last, the lesson came to an end. Jody had never been so relieved to hear that it was time for math!

3

Over lunch, Jody asked Luisa to tell them more about the mysterious Frida.

"I don't believe it!" Brittany said loudly, before Luisa could reply. "Honestly, Jody, were you asleep, or did you flunk out of your first year of Spanish? Luisa told us all about Frida this morning!"

"Well, maybe the other people at this table would like to hear about her," Jody shot back, thinking quickly. But she could feel herself flushing.

"Who's Frida?" Gina asked, seeing an argument brewing.

"My best friend," Luisa said solemnly. Then her eyes crinkled as she smiled warmly and confessed, "I'm afraid I was teasing the girls a little. Actually, Frida is a dolphin who lives in the waters I patrol. She's a very special dolphin, and I know you are all going to want to meet her."

Jody's eyes widened in surprise.

"I never met a dolphin I didn't like," Craig said with a grin, as he helped himself to salad. "But what's so special about this Frida?"

"She's a hybrid," Luisa replied. "A cross between a bottle-nosed and an Atlantic spotted dolphin!"

Craig gave a low whistle. "I'd heard that such cross-breeds were possible, but I've never seen one."

"That *is* something, all right," Gina said. "I certainly do want to meet her!"

"Me, too!" Jody said excitedly. She piled salad onto her own plate and passed the bowl. "How did you find her?" she asked Luisa. "And how did you know what kind she was?"

"I first saw her about a year ago, when I came to live on *Amigo del Mar*," Luisa replied, smiling.

"That means 'Friend of the Sea,'" Brittany informed Jody with a superior smile.

"I know that!" Jody snapped. She caught her mother's disapproving look, but she couldn't help herself. Brittany had found one area where she was better than Jody, and she sure was making the most of it!

Luisa ignored their bickering. "The dolphin came up to me while I was swimming one day," she explained. "I was very surprised! I didn't try to approach her or touch her — WDPL advises never to do that — but Frida kept coming back. She seemed very curious about me, and she soon made it clear that she wanted to be friends. She was a solitary dolphin — I never saw her with a group — and she enjoyed my company. This sort of thing happens from time to time, you know, solitary dolphins making friends with people, but usually the *solitarios* are male."

"I'd like to hear more about your work, Luisa," said Maddie. "Isn't Mexico *the* major dealer in dolphins for the display industry throughout Latin America?"

"That is true, I'm sorry to say," Luisa replied sadly. "Not only does my country keep more dolphins in captivity than any other single nation — often in dreadful conditions — but it also acts as a sort of 'middleman' by allowing dolphins captured in the wild to be sold out of Mexico."

"Why?" Jody asked, her food forgotten as she listened.

Luisa turned to her. "Well, you see, some countries have much tighter regulations than others about trading in dolphins," she explained. "Many simply don't allow any dolphins to be imported, whether they were caught in the wild or born in captivity. But sadly, other countries are all too willing to buy dolphins from places like Mexico without asking too many questions about their origin."

"But that's wrong!" Jody exclaimed.

Luisa nodded her agreement. "Yes, of course it is. The laws in Mexico about importing and exporting dolphins must be changed. But that won't happen until enough people understand that capturing wild dolphins is a cruel business that must be stopped."

"So why aren't *you* in Mexico?" Brittany asked.

Jody winced. Brittany's blunt question sounded

rude. But Jody had been wondering the very same thing.

Brittany flushed slightly, looking embarrassed. "I'm sorry . . . I'm not criticizing . . ." she added quickly. "It's just that you sound so passionate about it, and, after all, it is your country, so I thought you'd want to be there, trying to change the laws."

Luisa smiled at Brittany. "That's okay. It's a good question. I have worked in Mexico, and I will again. And I am trying to change things there, wherever I can. I write letters to people who matter. And I write and translate articles for Mexican newspapers and magazines. Sometimes I get letters from people saying that something I've written has changed their minds, or they've joined an animal welfare organization because of my words. That makes me feel good. But when I started work for the Whale and Dolphin Protection League, I agreed to go wherever they sent me. And for now, that's Jamaica. The waters around nearby Cuba are a notorious capture location."

"What does that mean?" Sean asked, frowning. "Who gets captured?"

"Pirates?" Jimmy suggested, his freckled face hopeful.

Luisa laughed and shook her head. "I'm talking about dolphins," she reminded the boys. "A lot of dolphins are captured in the sea around Cuba and then exported all over the world."

"And you're there to stop them?" Sean asked eagerly.

"Like a policeman?" said Jimmy. "Do you get to arrest the dolphin thieves?"

Luisa's smile was wistful. "I wish! Unfortunately, it's not that simple." She sighed, her shoulders drooping. "The reason so many dolphins are taken from those waters is that it's very easy to get dolphin capture permits from Cuba. So alas, it's perfectly legal," she said.

"But it's wrong!" Jody said fiercely. She'd lost her appetite altogether, now.

"But surely there's something you can do," Craig said, frowning. "Otherwise, why would the WDPL bother to station a boat there?"

"I'm there to monitor the captures, so we stay informed about how many dolphins are being taken from the area. That's not information the Cuban government necessarily wants to give out, you see," Luisa explained. "Also, I'm conducting a population study to get some idea of the size of the dolphin population in those waters."

Jody noticed that Dr. Taylor seemed to perk up and take an interest when Luisa mentioned the population study. He looked like he wanted to ask a question, but his mouth was full. By the time he'd finished chewing, the conversation had moved on.

After he'd finished eating, Craig went up to take over the helm from Harry.

"Hey, Dad — can Sean and I help you sail?" Jimmy asked.

"Sure, if you've finished eating, come on!" Craig called back.

The two boys went scrambling after him.

A few moments later, Harry came down the hatch and took a place at the table.

"Here, let me give you some salad," Luisa offered.

"Thanks," the captain replied gruffly.

"How much longer do we have to sail?" Luisa asked.

Harry shrugged. "We should reach the northeast

37

coast of Jamaica by tomorrow," he told her. "Or the next day . . . Why don't you radio to your boat and get the precise coordinates? Then I can give you a better estimate."

"What a good idea!" Luisa exclaimed. "Do you mind if I do that now? Or later . . . I don't want to interrupt your lunch," she added apologetically.

Harry glanced across at Jody and Brittany, then turned back to Luisa. "One of the girls can show you to the control room," he said.

"I'm done," Jody said quickly, standing up. "I'll show you."

"Thanks, Jody," Luisa replied, getting up, too. She followed her to the small, forward cabin where the radio, charts, and navigational equipment were kept. She nodded at the sight of the radio. "Yes, it's just like mine — I know how to use it."

Although Luisa didn't need her help, Jody hovered curiously. She heard Luisa make contact with a man called Frank. She knew that Frank also worked for the WDPL; he'd taken Luisa's place while she was away.

After Luisa had taken the coordinates, jotting them

on the palm of her hand with a pen, she said, "How are things there?"

"Not good." The man's voice sounded grim.

Luisa caught her breath. "What's been happening?"

The reply came: "A capture boat took four dolphins yesterday."

"Oh, no," Luisa groaned. Then she asked urgently, "What about Frida?"

"I don't know," said the man. "I was too far away to see anything except to count four dolphins taken. All I know is that I haven't seen any sign of Frida since yesterday morning. I haven't seen her since the capture boat left."

"Oh, Frank, no!" Luisa cried. Her face had gone pale, and she clenched her fists tightly.

The radio crackled, then the signal cleared. The voice came again. "I'm sorry, Luisa . . ."

September 16 — after bedtime — Still at sea.
I'm writing this under the cover in my bunk, so Brittany won't complain about the light. She takes every chance she gets to bother me. I thought that we were finally get-

ting to be more like friends. It seems I was wrong. So, she's better than me at speaking Spanish. Big deal. She's dyslexic, so I'm better than her at anything to do with reading and writing. Only I am too nice to rub her face in the things she can't do! Well, if she keeps pushing, maybe I won't always be so nice.

A squall blew up just after dinner, and I can hear the rain lashing down outside. I can't help thinking about poor Harry wrapped in his waterproof gear, outside at the helm in this awful weather!

And poor Luisa, so worried about Frida. She looked so sad, I wished I could say something to make her feel better. Oh, I hope Frida will turn out to be all right!

It was late afternoon the following day when *Dolphin Dreamer* entered Jamaican waters. The island of Jamaica appeared as little more than a misty smudge on the horizon, but Harry told them they were nearing the shallower waters where *Amigo del Mar* was currently lying at anchor.

Luisa stood anxiously at the side, gazing out at the empty, gray-green ocean. Jody watched her, wondering if she was hoping to spot one solitary dolphin swimming alone through the choppy waves.

It was a warm, windy day. There had been no rain since dawn, but the pale sky was full of racing clouds, and some of them looked dark and threatening.

"Ship ahoy," shouted Sean, and a second later, his brother's voice chimed in.

Jody shielded her eyes and squinted. After a moment, she saw something. Yes, there was definitely a

The Amigo Del Mar — *Luisa's home*

boat rocking gently on the water. "Is that your boat?" she asked Luisa.

Luisa caught her breath, then nodded vigorously. "Yes . . . I think so . . . yes!" A smile broke across her face. "Home," she said softly.

Soon, *Dolphin Dreamer* drew up alongside *Amigo del Mar*, and Harry barked out orders as Cam, Craig, and Gina dashed about taking in the sails. Next to the elegant lines of *Dolphin Dreamer*, the WDPL boat looked small and tubby, like a scruffy pony beside a thoroughbred racehorse.

Frank, a tall, balding Canadian with a thin, worried face, welcomed them aboard. He seemed startled, and blushed when Luisa threw her arms around him and gave him a big hug.

"Has Frida turned up yet?" she demanded anxiously as soon as she let him go.

He shook his head. "No, I'm sorry, Luisa. I haven't seen her." Then he looked past her, to the others who had boarded. "Hi, I'm Frank Cain, WDPL," he introduced himself.

"Craig McGrath," said Craig, shaking his hand. "This

is my wife, Gina, our daughter, Jody, and our assistant, Maddie. You'll meet the others when you come over for dinner later. I hope you *will* join us for dinner?"

Frank smiled, looking more relaxed. "Thanks. It'll be a treat to have a break from my own lousy cooking!"

Jody noticed that Luisa was still scanning the water, looking for Frida. She swallowed hard, feeling a lump in her throat, as she saw Luisa turn away, finally, her shoulders drooping.

"So, what's the news, Frank?" Luisa asked, her voice flat and listless.

"I heard from one of our contacts in Havana that the four dolphins have been put onto a plane bound for Mexico," he told her.

Luisa winced. "An ordinary commercial flight?"

Frank nodded unhappily. "Yes, and apparently there was no vet with them. It doesn't sound as if the dolphins were being handled as carefully as they should have been."

Luisa looked even more miserable. "So much for my speech at the Nassau conference!" she exclaimed. Glancing at Jody and the others, she explained, "I was trying to get all the airlines to refuse to transport dolphins except when absolutely necessary. And then, only to do so on dedicated flights, with a vet or some other expert on hand the whole time."

"Some airlines have already agreed," Frank consoled her.

"Yes, but not all of them," Luisa replied with a sigh. "Luckily it's only a short flight to Mexico; otherwise I'd be really afraid they wouldn't survive the journey!" She frowned. "Any idea where they're going?"

Frank shook his head. "No. But the flight was bound for Acapulco, so I've been in touch with Yolanda. She's promised to get someone to check out their importation documents at the airport, and she'll get back to us." A little awkwardly, he patted her shoulder. "There's nothing more we can do now, Luisa. We'll have to wait to hear more. Come on, let's show our visitors around, okay?"

Amigo del Mar might be small and shabby compared to *Dolphin Dreamer*, but there was something very friendly about it, Jody thought. The cabin below deck was decorated with photographs of smiling people. Luisa explained these were her friends and relatives back in Mexico.

Jody also noticed a photograph of a dolphin. The photographer had caught the dolphin in graceful motion, suspended above the dark blue sea. At first, Jody decided it must be a bottle-nosed dolphin. Then she realized that the dolphin's body and head seemed slightly less rounded than that of a bottle-nosed — more like an Atlantic spotted dolphin. And, as she looked more closely, Jody could see spots on the dolphin's paler belly. "Is this a picture of Frida?" she asked.

Luisa nodded, wordless. Her eyes were bright with tears.

Jody wished now she hadn't said anything to remind Luisa of her loss. Impulsively, she put her arms around the young woman and hugged her. "She'll be all right," she said earnestly. "I just know she will!" As Jody spoke, she hoped she was right.

Dolphin Dreamer spent that night anchored beside *Amigo del Mar.* The next day at breakfast, Harry announced his plans to sail to the nearest town so that

Mei Lin could stock up on fresh food. He offered to take Frank, too, since he was eager to get back to his own work on the mainland now that Luisa had returned.

"Can we go, too?" Jimmy asked, as usual speaking for his brother as well as himself.

"I think you'd better stay with us on *Amigo*," Gina began.

"Why?" Jimmy demanded. "It's Saturday, so there's no schoolwork."

"Harry's going to have enough to do without looking after you two," Gina explained.

Jimmy and Sean looked mutinous.

Then Cam came to the rescue. "I don't mind looking after them," he volunteered, with his charming smile. "We could have fun — they need a break."

"We all do," Jody muttered to herself. *Dolphin Dreamer* might be big compared to *Amigo del Mar*, but it was still too small a space to be cooped up with two energetic eight-year-olds for days on end.

Gina smiled. "Thanks, Cam, that would be terrific!"

she said warmly, her voice nearly drowned out by cheers from the twins.

"How about you, sweetheart?" Harry asked, with a tentative smile at Brittany. "How about a day out in Jamaica with your old man?"

Brittany shrugged. "Sure, why not?" she agreed, her expression carefully blank.

At least Brittany pretending she didn't care was an improvement over her old hostility, Jody thought. It might be fun to visit Jamaica, but right now, Jody was more interested in Luisa's plan to take those who wanted to go on a tour of the area to see what dolphins remained.

When Jody boarded *Amigo* a few minutes later with her parents, Maddie, and Dr. Taylor, she noticed immediately that Luisa was looking tense and angry.

"We've had news from one of our contacts in Mexico," she told them right away. "The dolphins have been taken to a new hotel complex in a coastal town not far from Acapulco."

Craig and Gina exchanged a worried look.

"Why would a hotel buy four dolphins?" Maddie asked, looking puzzled.

"For *entertainment*," Luisa said, with a sarcastic emphasis on the word. She shook her head angrily. "They've put the dolphins into what sounds like a really small pool located inside a bar-restaurant, for the amusement of the customers. There's nonstop loud music, night and day, and there's absolutely no supervision — the customers already seem to do as they please: tease the dolphins, throw drinks at them, drop trash into the pool, even get into the pool themselves. It sounds like the sort of place I wouldn't want to spend five minutes in, and those poor dolphins are going to be stuck there all the time, with no relief!" Her eyes gleamed with furious tears.

Jody was horrified. "Can't you rescue them?" she asked. "There must be something you can do!"

Luisa shook her head. "They were legally imported, so we can't remove them," she explained.

"But surely, if they're being mistreated — they can't get away with that! There are international laws against cruelty to animals," Gina said. Her face was pale with anger, and her hands were clenched tightly, as if she would have liked to punch the person responsible.

Beside her, Craig and Maddie were frowning. Even Dr. Taylor, nervously stroking his chin, looked shocked.

Luisa nodded agreement. "Yes. We'll mount a campaign immediately, on that basis. And, maybe, eventually, the hotel could be forced to make some changes . . . increase the size of the pool, put a fence around it and a guard to keep people and trash out . . . things like that," she finished.

"But that's not good enough!" Craig burst out furiously. "The dolphins shouldn't be there at all!"

"I feel exactly the same way," Luisa said quietly. "The situation is absolutely horrific. But, unfortunately, it all appears to be completely legal. The men who caught the dolphins had a permit from the Cuban government to do so. They were legally imported into Mexico and legally purchased by the hotel, which has been granted a license by the local authorities to keep dolphins on the premises. It's all totally wrong, of course, but we don't have a legal leg to stand on. All we can do is argue against the cruelty of their situation, insisting that they should be released if not kept in better conditions."

A gloomy silence fell as Luisa stopped speaking.

Then the unmistakable sound of a dolphin's whistle caught their attention. It was followed by a series of chattering clicks, along with sounds of splashing in the water on the starboard — or right — side of the boat.

Luisa caught her breath, and a wondering look lit up her face. "Frida?" she gasped.

She ran to the side of the boat. Jody and her parents were right behind.

There in the water, poking its head right up to look back at them, was a dolphin. It had the coloring of a bottle-nosed dolphin, the back and head a uniform steely gray.

Only when it reared up out of the water, as if considering leaping right over the boat, could Jody see that this dolphin was like no bottle-nosed she had ever seen before. Her underside was mottled and spotted with patches of lighter gray and white, revealing her mixed parentage.

"Oh, Frida, *querida!*" Luisa exclaimed. She had been

wearing a swimsuit with a sarong wrapped and tied into a sort of dress. Now, with a quick movement, she pulled the sarong off, kicked off her rubber-soled sandals, then leaped over the side of the boat into the water to join her friend.

4

Jody found herself blinking away tears of happiness as she leaned over the side to watch Luisa and Frida swimming together.

It was obvious that the dolphin had missed Luisa just as much as Luisa had missed her. Frida rubbed affectionately against Luisa, reminding Jody of a big cat. The sight of them swimming and playing together so happily made Jody think with a pang of longing of Apollo, the wild dolphin who had befriended her just off the coast of Florida at the beginning of their journey.

Luisa did not stay in the water very long.

"Please excuse me," she said, rather breathlessly, as Craig and Gina helped her back into the boat. "I know it was rude to desert you like that, but I simply *had* to greet Frida, after being so worried about her."

"There's nothing to apologize for," Gina said warmly. "We understand."

"Yes, of course you do," Luisa replied, smiling gratefully as Maddie managed to find her a dry towel.

"I would love to get some scenes of you and Frida together on video," Gina said. "Maybe later, if that's all right with you?"

Luisa nodded in agreement as she patted herself dry. "Yes, certainly. This afternoon, perhaps?"

"I'd especially like to film underwater," Gina added. "But that would have to be another day, since I left my scuba gear on board *Dolphin Dreamer.*"

Luisa looked a little uncertain. "The visibility here is not as great as you'd have found it in the Bahamas, so you may have to get pretty close . . . but you are both very experienced with filming dolphins, after all, so it would probably be okay."

Jody thought her father looked surprised that Luisa

seemed uncertain. "Frida seems to be a very friendly dolphin," he said. "Do you think our presence would bother her?"

"Probably not," she said. "But not all her experiences with people have been good ones. She has a terrible jagged scar on her belly, most likely caused by a boat propeller . . . you'll see it when you are in the water with her. She is much more cautious around boats other than *Amigo del Mar*, and she should be! She shouldn't forget that not all people can be trusted — for her own safety."

"Otherwise, there's a good chance she'll be captured," Maddie added, grimly.

Luisa nodded. "Yes, this is a dangerous area for dolphins. Cuba gives out far too many capture permits for these waters. Really, they should conduct a scientific study of the local dolphin population. You see," she went on, roughly drying her hair, "there are international regulations which forbid the capture of bottle-nosed dolphins unless it has been *proven* that taking individual dolphins from a particular area won't be too harmful to the remaining population."

"How does that work?" Jody asked.

"Well, you see," Luisa explained, "if there are plenty of dolphins in an area, then it doesn't matter so much if a few are taken. I mean, it matters to the dolphins, of course," she added with a grimace. "And it matters to me. But a scientist might look at a group and decide that it would still survive if it lost ten, or even twenty, dolphins. However, the same scientist could also decide that another group might die out altogether if only five are taken away."

Craig nodded. "And the survival of a group also depends on *which* of the dolphins are taken," he commented.

"That's right," Luisa agreed. "The display industry wants only the strongest, healthiest animals, and if too many of these are taken, the remaining dolphins are often too old or too sick to reproduce. So the survival of the group is endangered."

Jody stared at her. "But . . . I didn't think the bottle-nosed dolphin was an endangered species!" she exclaimed.

Luisa shook her head reassuringly. "No, it's not. And

we hope it never will be. That's why laws were passed, to help stop that from happening. Once the number of dolphins in an area falls below a certain level, capture has to be banned."

Gina nodded. "So, because dolphin capture is so profitable, and because setting up a scientific population research study also costs money, the Cuban government has decided to *assume* that the local population is still big and healthy, instead of investigating it properly?"

Luisa pointed her finger like a pistol. "You got it," she agreed.

Dr. Taylor, who had been quietly listening, now frowned thoughtfully. "But, Señorita Suarez, I thought you mentioned earlier that *you* were conducting a population study?"

Luisa nodded. "Yes, I have been trying to . . . Sponsored by the WDPL, not the Cuban government." She sighed. "There is a problem, though. I'm not really qualified. I have no scientific training. The League hired a researcher a few months ago, but, unfortunately, they ran out of funds before the research was complete. After she left, I tried to continue the study as best I could. We have masses of data, but I've been too busy with other things to organize and analyze it all properly," she finished apologetically.

"I'd very much like to have a look at whatever data you do have," Dr. Taylor said eagerly.

Luisa smiled at him. "You're welcome to it — but I should warn you, it's a mess . . . it might take you a while to get through it all . . ."

Dr. Taylor rubbed his hands together. "Well, as long as we're here, I should get started," he said happily. He patted the case in which he carried his laptop. "I might even be able to help you analyze your data," he told Luisa. "Before I left, my company supplied me with what's supposed to be the most advanced number-crunching program on the market . . . but I haven't had anything sufficiently challenging to try it out on!"

"Well, that would certainly be helpful," Luisa agreed, smiling. "Come on, Dr. Taylor, I'll get you settled at my desk down below."

The McGraths and Maddie watched in amazement as Dr. Taylor followed Luisa.

Was he finally going to do something useful? Or was

this just another one of his excuses for getting out of the hot sun and having a snooze? Jody wondered. She found her dad looking at her.

He grinned as if he knew what she was thinking, then said quietly, "It would be a dull old world if everybody liked exactly the same things. Who knows, maybe Dr. Taylor will surprise us someday."

"I doubt *that* very much!" Jody replied with a snort of disbelief.

A short while later, Luisa started up the boat's engine and took them out on a short patrol. While Dr. Taylor looked through the research findings in the cabin, Jody stayed on deck with her parents and Maddie. She enjoyed the feel of the wind in her hair as she scanned the waves for any sign of the familiar, curving fins that meant dolphins.

Frida followed them for a time, leaping into the air in a way that seemed to demonstrate her happiness. Then she swam away from the boat and disappeared, and they saw no sign of her for the next few hours.

Late in the afternoon, they returned to the spot

where *Amigo* had been anchored, its position marked by a floating orange and white buoy. Jody was disappointed that during the whole day they'd seen only one group of bottle-nosed dolphins, and it had kept its distance, showing no interest in approaching the boat.

But her disappointment vanished as soon as she looked over the side and was rewarded by the sight of a friendly dolphin face gazing up at her.

"Hey, Luisa, Frida's back!" Jody called out happily.

Luisa came out of the engine house, smiling and unbuttoning the long overshirt she had put on earlier. "She's waiting for me to come in for my afternoon swim," she explained.

Jody couldn't hold back. "Could I go swimming with her, too?" she asked.

Luisa's expression immediately became guarded. She didn't reply right away.

Not understanding this, Jody cast a glance at her mother.

"Jody has been swimming with dolphins before," Gina said. "She knows how to behave, if that's what you're worried about. Her father and I trust her completely," she assured Luisa. "But if you'd rather she didn't . . ."

Jody's heart sank.

But then Luisa began to relax again. Slowly, she nodded. "It's not really up to me to decide. We'll just have to see how *Frida* feels about making a new friend!"

She patted Jody's arm. "Go get your swimsuit on, and we'll swim together."

A few minutes later, Jody dived off the side of the boat. The water was cooler than she'd been used to during the summer in the Bahamas, but it felt great as she plunged in.

She popped up to the surface, and wiped the water from her eyes. Looking around, she saw Luisa treading water and talking softly in Spanish to Frida. The dolphin kept nudging against Luisa, making her laugh.

Watching their closeness, seeing the affection between them, made Jody envious. She waited for Frida to come and introduce herself, but the dolphin showed no interest in leaving her friend, not even when Luisa turned toward Jody and seemed to urge Frida in her direction.

Jody thought of her own first dolphin friend, Apollo, and wondered what he was doing now. She wished she could see him swimming with his group, leaping and diving and enjoying life in the way that came naturally to wild dolphins.

With an effort, Jody shook off the sadness that threatened. She wanted to make friends with Frida, but she knew this was something that couldn't be forced. Taking a deep breath, she began to swim. She decided to make her way around *Amigo del Mar.* It felt great to stretch her muscles and glide through the waves, although it wasn't as easy as she had expected. She hadn't been swimming for several days, as they had been in too much of a hurry to get down to Jamaica to stop on the way.

She was on her second lap around the boat when she realized she wasn't alone. Someone was swimming alongside her, keeping pace with her. Jody turned her head, expecting to see Luisa. But it was Frida!

Jody was so startled by the sight of the dolphin that she breathed in when she shouldn't have, and choked on a gulp of salt water.

Making friends with Frida

She began to cough.

Frida came closer, close enough to touch — but Jody didn't even think about it. She couldn't seem to stop coughing. Her eyes were streaming. She pounded herself on the chest and struggled to breathe normally. It was hard, because a sudden breeze had made the water choppier. She had to keep churning her arms and legs to keep her head high enough above the water to avoid another wave washing into her mouth. She was tiring rapidly.

And then, to her astonishment, she felt a smooth, strong body pressing against her, lifting her up. Frida had noticed her struggles and was helping her out — just like Apollo had done when Jody had fallen over-board from *Dolphin Dreamer!*

Gratefully, Jody let herself rest against the dolphin. She took the support she was offered. As she rested, her breathing quickly got back to normal. As soon as she had recovered, she moved away. She didn't want to restrict Frida in any way.

But Frida showed no desire to leave. She gazed at Jody sidelong out of one round, intelligent eye.

Jody gazed back, fascinated, feeling once again the marvelous sense of peace and safety, which the nearness of dolphins always gave her. There was no need for words. Somehow she felt they understood each other.

Luisa came swimming up beside them. "Good. I see you two have made friends," she said, smiling.

5

September 20 — bedtime, anchored off the coast of Jamaica.

Mom and Dad say that we must set sail again tomorrow. Brittany has been moaning because she wants another day or two "on vacation" with her dad ashore in Jamaica. She has been a little bit nicer to me lately because she's having a good time, but as soon as things are back to normal I bet she'll start sniping at me again.

I'm going to get up really early in the morning and see if I can have one last swim with Frida before we go. It'll be hard to leave her and Luisa, but when I think of all the *amazing dolphins (and whales) we are bound to meet further south . . . well . . . I can't wait!*

When Jody emerged from her cabin early the next morning — leaving Brittany still yawning and groaning in her bunk — she was surprised to discover Luisa already in the main cabin with her parents.

". . . so that's why I need to go right away," Luisa said.

"At least you can stay for breakfast," Gina said firmly. "I'll go see if Mei Lin's started cooking yet."

Jody raised her eyebrows. "*You're* leaving?" she asked Luisa as her mother went out. "Why? Where are you going?"

"I'm going to Mexico," Luisa told her. "I was just explaining to your parents . . . Frank can't cover for me this time, so I'll have to leave *Amigo* in dock."

Then Jody noticed how worried Luisa looked. "What's happened?" she asked. "Is it something about the dolphins?"

Luisa nodded. "One of the four dolphins has died."

"Oh, no!" Jody cried, horrified.

"I'm afraid so," Luisa replied sadly. "So now it's even

more urgent that I try to save the other three. As I just told your parents, WDPL is paying my travel expenses. They want me to try to convince the owner to release the remaining dolphins before it is too late for them."

Craig ran a hand over his unshaven face, frowning with concern. "Why did it die? Any idea?"

Luisa shook her head. "I'll need to talk to the local vet," she said. "And I'll know more when I see for myself how they're being kept . . . I would guess that the shock of being captured — dolphin-catchers can be brutal! — followed by the stress of the flight to Mexico, was too much. I'm worried in case any of the others have been injured. Even though they've survived so far, their resistance to infection will have been lowered by stress," she explained. "The pool where they are being kept sounds like a very unhealthy place."

Gina came out of the galley with mugs of coffee on a tray. She handed one to Luisa. "Mei Lin's slicing oranges and warming some rolls," she said. "I know you don't want to waste any time, but you shouldn't go racing off without something to eat."

Luisa smiled at her. "Thanks, Gina," she said gratefully. "I should take you along to look after me!" She sipped her coffee and sighed with pleasure. "Ah, I need this. I've been up most of the night talking to different people on the radio, trying to sort things out."

Jody chewed her lip anxiously. "What if you can't talk the owners into setting them free?" she asked.

"Well, I'll try to persuade local people to protest," Luisa said. She sighed and shook her head. "But the hotel owner may not care what local people think if he makes his money on tourists. As long as there are tourists willing to come and spend money to see the dolphins, he won't want to lose them."

"So what you really need to do is get hotel customers to tell the owner that they won't come again unless he gets rid of the dolphins," Jody said eagerly.

Luisa nodded. "Yes, of course. But that sort of campaign could take years," she replied, frustratedly. "I want to help those dolphins *now*."

Dr. Taylor entered the main cabin, rubbing his eyes sleepily. "Did I smell coffee?" he asked hopefully. "Is breakfast ready?"

"Mei Lin's just started cooking," Gina told him. "But sit down and I'll get you a cup of coffee."

"Thank you kindly," he said. He put his laptop on the table. "If no one objects, I'll just check my e-mail while we're waiting to eat."

As he sat down, he noticed Luisa. "Señorita Suarez!" he exclaimed, looking startled. "Good morning! Although I was working until very late last night, I'm afraid I still haven't managed to transfer all your data. I hope you didn't come here expecting —"

Luisa waved a hand to cut him off. "No, no, Doctor," she said soothingly. "I wasn't even thinking of that. I'm afraid I have some bad news which means I have to fly to Mexico right away."

"I wish *we* could help!" Jody burst out, when Luisa had filled Dr. Taylor in on what had happened.

"Maybe we can," Craig said, looking thoughtful.

They all looked at him.

"Well, I was just thinking," he began. "Dolphin Universe is partly about educating the public. We might be able to help by spreading the word about what is happening to these dolphins."

Gina nodded enthusiastically. "You could supply us with some firsthand information," she told Luisa. "If you send us some photos, we could post them on the website. Any chance you might have access to a video camera?"

Luisa shook her head. "Even if I rented one, I wouldn't know how to use it! I'm afraid I'm pretty useless with all that stuff."

Gina frowned. "What a shame. If I had some good video footage, I'll bet WDOL-TV in Florida would use it. It's the sort of story they would love."

Jody's thoughts were leaping ahead. "And then other TV stations in other cities might pick it up," she added. "If enough Americans see the video and write to protest, maybe that hotel owner would decide that having the dolphins was keeping tourists away, and he'd agree to release them!" She beamed at Luisa excitedly. "Don't you think that's a good idea?"

"It's a great idea," Luisa agreed, smiling wryly. She shook her head. "But as I said, unlike Gina, I don't have a video camera. And I don't know how to use one . . ." She hesitated. Something seemed to spark in her dark eyes.

Suddenly, she leaned forward and spoke urgently to Gina. "You could come with me! Bring your video camera, and get the facts for yourself — and tell them to the world!"

Jody held her breath, watching as her parents exchanged a glance.

But Gina shook her head regretfully. "I'd love to, Luisa, but how could I get to the other side of Mexico from here? It would take us weeks to sail there, and our budget wouldn't cover airfares . . ." She paused uncertainly. "I don't suppose your organization would fund my travel?"

Luisa shook her head. "The money for mine came out of the emergency campaign fund. It won't stretch much further," she said sadly.

"I really am sorry," Gina said. She reached across the table to touch Luisa's hand. "I wish I could go with you. If only it were possible . . ."

"It *might* be possible," said Dr. Jefferson Taylor.

They all looked at him in surprise. Jody had practically forgotten he was there, tapping away at his laptop.

"What do you mean?" Craig asked.

Dr. Taylor pointed a stubby forefinger at the computer screen. "I've just heard from my employers," he said. "They don't feel they're getting their money's worth out of their sponsorship . . ."

"What do they expect?" Craig demanded, frowning. "We're not wasting their money; we're doing exactly what we said we were going to do."

"Yes, yes, I agree! I'm not complaining myself!" Dr. Taylor waved his hands nervously. "I was just trying to compose a reply to explain that, but now I've had a better idea." He paused and smiled a little hesitantly. "You see, PetroCo wants more publicity. They'd like to see more about Dolphin Universe — sponsored by PetroCo — in the press and on TV. Dr. McGrath's idea of publicizing the captive dolphins in Mexico sounds perfect." He nodded at Gina. "I will suggest to them that they fund your travel expenses so you can go to Mexico and launch a campaign — a highly newsworthy, visible, public campaign — to free the dolphins." He hesitated, peering anxiously at Gina. "That is, if you agree."

Gina smiled. "Dr. Taylor, I think that is an absolutely wonderful idea," she said warmly.

Luisa, too, was smiling broadly. She jumped up and leaned over to plant a kiss on Dr. Taylor's cheek. *"Muchas gracias,"* she thanked him. "You are a very dear, thoughtful man!"

Turning bright red, Dr. Taylor did not reply. Hunched over his keyboard, he quickly wrote a letter to his employers.

Dr. Taylor — speechless for once!

September 21 — just before dinner. Still anchored near Jamaica.

Still no reply from PetroCo! But Luisa is so convinced that "dear Dr. Taylor" will get his way that she has delayed her flight from Kingston to Acapulco until first thing tomorrow, and she reserved a place for Mom, too. While they're gone, we'll stay here and keep an eye on things — so it seems I won't be saying good-bye to Frida just yet, after all!

The cabin door opened and Brittany stuck her head in. "Hurry up," she said bossily. "Dinner's almost ready, and Dr. Taylor is about to make an announcement — though why everyone has to wait for you, I can't imagine."

Jody didn't pause to argue. Quickly, she stashed her diary away, rolled off her bunk, and hurried to join the others at the big table in the main cabin.

Dr. Taylor looked like he was enjoying everyone's suspense. But after clearing his throat several times, he finally said, "I'm pleased to tell you that PetroCo thinks it's a splendid idea! My employer has recently suffered from some bad publicity connected with an oil spill in the Mediterranean. They think that publicity showing PetroCo as a 'friend of the dolphins' would be really helpful at this rather difficult time. So, they have agreed to pay all the expenses for two members of Dolphin Universe to travel to Mexico and back."

Jody sighed with relief.

But Gina looked a little apprehensive. "So, Luisa and I will have the pleasure of your company, Dr. Taylor?" she asked.

"Me?" Dr. Taylor looked alarmed.

"Well, I assumed when you said two, that you —" Gina began.

"Oh, no, no, no!" Dr. Taylor exclaimed, shaking his head. "Air travel doesn't agree with me . . . and anyway, I can't possibly go to Mexico — not now! I have this dolphin population study to finish, all this research data to analyze . . . I really can't leave at this stage. No, no, Dr. McGrath — surely you'd rather be accompanied by your husband?"

"It makes more sense for me to stay and look after things here," Craig said, regretfully. "Anyway, Gina doesn't need me getting in the way of her video camera," he joked.

Then Luisa spoke up. "Maybe Jody should come with us," she suggested.

Jody could hardly believe her ears. She caught her breath with excitement and looked to see how her mother would respond.

"I'm sure Jody would be very helpful," Luisa added. "And it would be very educational for her." She smiled at Jody. "After all, if you're going to make your own career in working with dolphins, you need to understand some of the difficulties involved!"

"Oh, I'd love to go!" Jody exclaimed. She gazed pleadingly at her mother, hardly daring to hope.

Gina smiled back at her. "Well, since PetroCo has agreed to pay for *two* fares . . . why not? Luisa is right. Welcome to the rescue team, sweetheart!"

"Oh, wow! Thanks! This is so great — I'm so excited!" Jody jumped up and went to give her mother and Luisa hugs.

"But Jody — you should be prepared. You will see things that will make you sad and angry," Luisa said warningly. "Things you may be able to do nothing about."

Jody nodded to show she understood, but still, she couldn't help feeling excited. And she was sure that, between them, her mother and Luisa would work out a way to rescue the captive dolphins.

As she sat down for dinner, Jody noticed Brittany scowling at her.

"It's not fair," the other girl muttered. "She goes flying off to Mexico, while the rest of us have to stay here and do our schoolwork the same as always."

Maddie, who was sitting beside her, put a comforting hand on Brittany's shoulder and flashed a mischievous smile at Jody. "Don't fret, Britt," she advised. "I'll be expecting Jody to take advantage of this trip to work extra hard on her Spanish. And to make sure she does, I'm scheduling a test for the day she gets back!"

6

September 22 — morning, in a taxi — Mexico.
Seems like we've been traveling for an hour since we got this cab at the airport. Luisa said the Hotel Miramar was "just outside" Acapulco, but it must be much farther away than that! I think it took us less time to fly from Jamaica to Mexico than it's taking us to drive to the hotel!

All I can see out the window is boring old rocks and ground and scrubby plants by the side of the highway. And, occasionally, a little splash of bright blue. That's the Pacific Ocean! My first sight of it! In a few months we'll be sailing out there. But Mom and I are getting a sneak preview now!

"This looks like it," said Gina.

Jody looked up from her writing to see a huge pink-and-turquoise billboard advertising HOTEL MIRAMAR. Projecting out of the top of the billboard were the outlines of two leaping dolphins.

The taxi turned off the highway just after the sign. Moments later, it pulled to a stop in the curving driveway in front of a large, obviously new, pink stucco building. They got out and, after a rapid conversation in Spanish, Luisa paid the driver.

Jody followed her mother and Luisa through the double glass doors into reception. This was a spacious, pleasant area decorated with big flowerpots. A few people were sitting in deep, wicker chairs reading newspapers, and there was a pleasant smell of cinnamon, chocolate, and flowers in the air.

Luisa marched up to the front desk and identified herself. Moments later, a man in a white suit with carefully styled black hair came out to meet them. He spoke in Spanish to Luisa, who nodded, then turned to draw Gina and Jody into the conversation.

"Señor Martinez, these are my *compañeras*, Dr. Gina McGrath and her daughter, Jody," Luisa said.

"Ah, you are American?" Señor Martinez switched into speaking English as he noticed them. He sounded surprised. "So, do you also work for this dolphin protection league?"

"No," Gina replied. "I'm a marine biologist, representing an international research project known as Dolphin Universe. We have funding from various sources, including a television station in Florida." She held up her camcorder. "I'd like to take a video of the dolphins you have here, if you don't mind."

Jody held her breath. What if Señor Martinez said no?

But he smiled broadly, revealing brilliantly white teeth. "For American television?" he asked hopefully.

Gina nodded. "Yes, if they decide to use it, it will be shown in Florida, at least."

"Oh, I hope so," Señor Martinez said, clasping his hands in front of his chest. "If the people in Florida see my wonderful hotel, I am sure they will decide to come and stay here!"

"We're only here to film the dolphins, Señor Martinez," Luisa replied. "And it should interest you to know that most American tourists would boycott a hotel where dolphins were being mistreated," she added quietly.

The hotel owner looked indignant. "Certainly I don't mistreat *our* dolphins!" he exclaimed. "They have a lovely, deep pool to swim in, and we give them plenty to eat. I've spent a fortune to get these animals — why should I treat them badly? I am not a cruel man — ask anyone!"

Luisa nodded quickly. "Forgive me," she said, and gave him a dazzling smile.

Jody knew Luisa didn't want to anger Señor Martinez, in case he decided not to cooperate with them.

"I'm sure you wouldn't be deliberately cruel," Luisa continued. "But, after all, one of the dolphins has died already, so we are very worried. You see, it isn't easy to look after dolphins. It requires specialized knowledge."

Señor Martinez accepted Luisa's apology, and spoke cheerfully to Gina. "Maybe you could give me some advice. I always want to do what's best. Follow me and I'll show you the dolphins."

He took them outside through a back door, and along a concrete path that led downhill, toward a rocky beach. Jody saw the bright blue of the Pacific Ocean stretched out beneath the lighter blue of the cloudless sky. Gentle breakers rolled and splashed onto the shore.

But the peaceful, pleasant sound of the ocean was drowned out by a heavy, thumping bass beat. Loud music was playing somewhere, and it was getting louder as they approached. Jody realized that Señor Martinez was taking them to a building that was identified by a hot-pink neon sign as THE BEACH BAR.

"I am thinking of getting a new sign and renaming it The Dolphin Bar," the hotel owner explained as he ushered them in.

The bar was built on a semi-circular design, around a large, central patio that was open to the sky. Tables and chairs were scattered thickly around some sort of pool. Only about half a dozen of the tables were occupied at the moment.

Raising his voice to be heard above the pounding music, Señor Martinez said, "It's quiet now, but in the evening, it really fills up. There's a dance floor over on that side, and a video-game arcade inside at the back. And the bartenders can make any drink you want! Would you ladies like a drink?"

"No, thank you," Luisa replied. Gina shook her head firmly.

Jody thought they were wasting time. "Where are the dolphins?" she asked, shouting to make herself heard.

Señor Martinez looked at her in surprise. "There they are." He pointed. "In the pool."

A chill went through Jody. The pool was obviously too small for even one dolphin to live comfortably, let alone three. Jody walked toward it, staring in horrified disbelief as she took in every sordid detail.

The three dolphins huddled together in the cloudy, stagnant-looking water. Jody noticed a broken white Styrofoam cup floating on the surface, along with spent matchsticks and cigarette ends. On the concrete bottom she could see the gleam of small coins and other objects she couldn't make out. People must have thrown them in, she realized. She shuddered as she wondered what else got thrown into the pool with the dolphins, striking against their sensitive skin, bruising or wounding them.

Tears filled Jody's eyes. She turned away, unable to bear the sight of the dolphins in their misery. "Oh, the poor things!" she blurted out.

"Poor!" The hotel owner snorted indignantly. "Why, they've just had the most enormous fish breakfast! I'm the one who'll soon be poor if they always eat like that! If they don't look so lively now, it's because they're digesting their food."

"This pool is too small for them," Luisa told him, her voice wavering slightly as she took in the full horror of the situation. "And look, the water is filthy!" She bent down and plucked out the Styrofoam cup, which she used to scoop up some of the matches and cigarette ends.

Señor Martinez waved away her objections. "The boy who cleans the pool was late this morning," he explained. "He's done a good job, so far. Anyway, that's nothing. You think the ocean is so clean? It's full of pollution! Even more trash and filth. Here, we clean it out every day — the customers throw their trash in, what can you do?" He shrugged. "And once a week, a chlorine tablet is added to sterilize the water," he finished proudly.

Jody realized then that the strong smell she had noticed was chlorine. It smelled even stronger here than it did in the swimming pools at home.

Luisa's face was grim. "You know, dolphins are used to living in sea water," she told Señor Martinez. "Chemicals aren't good for them."

Señor Martinez frowned. "But health and safety regulations say we must put chlorine in the water," he declared. "I was very, very sad when the one dolphin died. I was afraid maybe the others would get an infection from it, so I put an extra chlorine tablet in, just to make sure all the germs were gone!" He flashed a smile at Gina. "You see, we have the same high standards as your American hotels. Only the best for my guests!"

"That was probably too much," Gina replied, biting her lip. "The smell is very strong, don't you agree? A little chlorine is useful, but too much isn't good for people or animals. It will hurt their eyes and burn their skin."

"Too much?" Señor Martinez raised his eyebrows and

shrugged. "Maybe, maybe. I will check the dosage. I always think it's better to be safe than sorry when it comes to germs. But of course, if too much could hurt them . . ." A look of concern flickered across his face. He said earnestly, "I don't want my dolphins to become sick. They were a big investment for me!"

"Señor Martinez, dolphins are large animals that need a lot of exercise to stay well," Luisa advised him. "If you really want to keep them healthy, they'll need more space. They need a much bigger pool, and cleaner water. And they should be able to escape from the customers to get a bit of peace . . ."

Señor Martinez snorted. "A bigger pool! Do you know how much that one cost? It is plenty big enough!" He shook his finger at her teasingly. "I think you really want me to put them back in the ocean, don't you? Admit it!"

"That's right!" Jody blurted out, before she could stop herself. "The dolphins will die if you keep them here! Look at them — you can see they're not well! They're so unhappy . . ." Jody faltered, worried that she might have offended Señor Martinez and turned him against them. Then she relaxed as the hotel owner's face broke into an indulgent smile.

He shook his head. "I don't think so, little one," he said. "Look, they are smiling! Such happy creatures are dolphins — happy all the time! I love to look at them." Then Señor Martinez's face turned serious. "And they won't die, I assure you," he added. "The veterinarian checked them over for me. I am taking good care of them." He paused and looked at his watch. "Now, if you will excuse me, I have much work . . ."

"Señor Martinez, please wait!" said Luisa urgently. "Could I speak to the vet myself?"

He nodded. "Certainly. Come to my office and I will phone him for you."

"I'm going to stay here and film," Gina said. "If that's all right?"

This produced a wide smile. "Yes! Certainly!" the hotel owner replied. He gestured around the bar. "Film everything! And if you'd like anything to eat or drink, just ask the bartender. It's on the house."

"Just one other thing, Señor Martinez," Gina added.

"Yes?" he asked.

"Do you think you could turn the music off, please? It's giving me a headache," she told him.

Señor Martinez frowned. "We never turn the music off, señora. The customers like it. Our motto is, *The Fun and the Music Never Stop!* But if you insist, I can lower the volume."

"Please," Gina replied. "I think the dolphins would appreciate it, too."

He looked puzzled. Then he laughed as if she had made a joke.

"Dolphins have very sensitive hearing, Señor Martinez," Luisa told him seriously as they walked away together. "An atmosphere like this is very stressful for them."

Jody watched her mother check the settings on her camera. After a few moments, the music became a little quieter.

Thankfully, Jody looked down at the dolphins again. Seeing them huddled together in the small, concrete pool made her stomach hurt, and her lungs felt so tight she could hardly breathe. She clutched at the little silver dolphin she wore on a chain around her neck.

From her conversations with Luisa, she knew that campaigns for the release of captive dolphins could often take years to be successful, and many dolphins died long before they could be set free.

"See if you can tempt any of the dolphins to swim over to you, honey," Gina called softly. "I'll have to come back this evening when there's lots of people so I can capture the real horror of the situation. But I'll take some shots now, too, while I've got the opportunity."

Jody was glad to be given something she could do to help. She went and sat on the edge of the pool, careful not to frighten them. In captivity, dolphins soon got used to people and were often trained to respond to visitors. But these dolphins were still wild, and she was a stranger.

She gazed down into the murky water and felt her heart go out to them. They must be feeling so strange, she thought. They were probably missing their friends in the ocean and mourning the one who had died. She wondered what ages they were and what relationship they had with each other.

As she wondered and watched, sitting quietly, the

dolphins moved out of their little huddle. The biggest one, a male, moved away from the other two and swam toward her. He broke the surface of the water with a tiny, explosive puff of air from his blowhole. Then he raised his whole head out of the water and looked at her. He swam the brief length of the pool, watching Jody the whole time, then flipped over and swam back again, still watching her.

Jody smiled but she didn't move. He was curious about her! "Hi, fella," she said quietly. "I'm Jody. What's your name?" She paused, hoping that he would whistle or click at her in response. But he just continued to swim and to watch her.

"I'm going to give you a name," she told him. "It's more friendly that way." She paused and looked hard at him to get some ideas.

He was a big, healthy-looking bottle-nosed dolphin. His back and sides were a sleek slate-gray color, and his underside was a paler gray. His skin was smooth and unmarked, without any scars. This made Jody think he must be pretty young. Over the years, dolphins picked up a lot of marks on their skins, not only scars from accidents, but also tooth marks made by other dolphins when they fought or played together.

"I know," she said suddenly. "I'll call you Chico!" *Chico* was the Spanish word for "boy" and was often used as a friendly nickname. Somehow, it seemed just right for this handsome young dolphin!

The other two dolphins swam over to join Chico in watching Jody. She could just make out a rapid clicking sound coming from one or both of them beneath the water. That gave her an idea, and she whistled, trying to make the sound that she remembered as Apollo's signature whistle.

Unfortunately, it seemed to get lost in the thumping bar music, which had grown louder again. Jody tried again, but she couldn't tell if the dolphins recognized what she was trying to do, or if they could even hear her whistle. She sighed with frustration.

Then she felt her mother's hands on her shoulders. She looked up.

"I'm going to find Luisa," Gina told her. "I need to make a couple of phone calls. Do you want to come with me, or wait for us here?"

Although The Beach Bar was a horrible place, Jody felt she was on the brink of making friends with the captive dolphins. She didn't want to abandon them so soon. "I'll stay here," she replied.

"Okay, sweetheart," her mother said, squeezing Jody's arm comfortingly. "We'll be back in a little while. If you get fed up, just come to the lobby and ask for me at the desk."

Jody turned her attention back to the dolphins. They were more active now, which seemed proof that they were in good condition. But it was heartbreaking to watch them cooped up in such a small pool, where they could only swim around and around in circles.

She blinked furiously, determined not to cry, and tried to concentrate on thinking up names for the other two dolphins. It was hard to be sure, but she thought they were both females. Their gray skins were just as smooth and unmarked as Chico's, so they were probably about the same age. And they were as alike as twins. Jody gazed at them, trying to see some small differences between them to give her ideas for names.

The sound of a voice made her look around. A girl

who looked about her own age, wearing an embroidered white dress and with her dark brown hair in braids, was standing beside the pool, smiling at her and talking to her — in Spanish.

Jody scrambled to her feet. She felt embarrassed. She couldn't understand a word.

The girl paused, still smiling. She was waiting for a reply.

Very glad that Brittany was not on hand to hear her mangled attempt at Spanish, Jody stammered out an apology, explaining that she didn't really speak Spanish: *"Lo siento mucho, pero yo no hablo español."*

"Oh! You are American?" the girl asked.

Jody sighed with relief and nodded.

"How do you do?" the girl asked. "My name is Carmelita."

"I'm Jody," she replied.

"Are you staying with your family here at the hotel?" Carmelita asked.

"Oh, no," Jody said quickly. "We're staying somewhere else. We just came here to see the dolphins."

Carmelita's eyes lit up. "Ah, the dolphins! They are

wonderful! The most wonderful thing ever to come to our town!" she exclaimed. "Don't you love them?" Smiling, she turned to gaze into the pool.

"Yes," Jody agreed. "I do love dolphins. My mom and dad are marine biologists; knowing about dolphins is their specialty."

"How wonderful!" Carmelita sighed. "I'd love to know more . . ." She leaned out over the pool. "Look, here comes Luna!"

One of the female dolphins swam up and rose out of the water, chattering. Then she plunged back down.

Carmelita laughed with delight. "I think she remembers me from yesterday!"

"Did you call her Luna?" Jody asked.

"Oh, that's just my name for her," Carmelita explained. "If you look at her closely, you can see a tiny little mark beside her eye, like a crescent moon. *Luna* means moon *en español*," she added.

"Of course," Jody said. She was impressed that the other girl had noticed such a tiny detail. "How about the others?" she asked. "Have you given them names?"

"Well, I call the other girl Chata," Carmelita said. She

Getting to know some new friends!

laughed and tossed her head, looking shy. "It's a pet name, I don't know how you would say it in English, but it's about this." She tapped her own small nose. "And it also means someone who is very cute . . ." She shrugged. "Anyway, I am still trying to think of a name for the big one."

"I called him Chico," Jody told her.

Carmelita beamed. "Okay, I like that!" she exclaimed. "Very good! Chico and Chata and Luna!" She sighed happily. "Look at them, smiling at us. I think they like their names."

Jody shook her head. "They're not smiling, Carmelita," she said gently. "That's just the shape their mouth makes. They look like that all the time — even when they're miserable. And, to be honest, I think they are pretty miserable right now."

Carmelita's smile faded. She stared at Jody in astonishment. "Why? Why do you say that?" she demanded, frowning.

So Jody told Carmelita why she had come to Mexico with her mother and Luisa. She explained about the sort of life that dolphins led in the wild, and pointed out how different the tiny, concrete, over-chlorinated pool was from the ocean they were meant to live in.

As she spoke, Jody watched Carmelita's expression gradually change from one of surprise and disbelief to one of concern and understanding. Jody was relieved.

Then Carmelita's expression turned to one of resolve. "I want to help you with your campaign," she told Jody firmly. "The dolphins must go home. We must make Señor Martinez understand that it is too cruel to keep them here like this. When I tell my father —"

"Jody!" The sound of her mother's voice made Jody turn around. She saw Gina and Luisa approaching.

"We're ready to leave, honey," Gina said.

"This is my mom," Jody told Carmelita. She introduced Gina and Luisa to her new friend.

Luisa greeted Carmelita in Spanish. The girl responded with a series of rapid questions. The Spanish was too quick for Jody to follow.

Carmelita turned to Jody, and then Gina. "I would like you all to come to my house, to tell my father about the dolphins. Please, won't you come?"

Gina looked at Luisa, who shook her head. "I'm

sorry, Carmelita," she said. "It's very kind of you, but we have a lot of work to do, to save the dolphins. It's already lunchtime —"

"You could eat at our house! There's always lots — you would be most welcome!" Carmelita interrupted.

Luisa shook her head again.

But before she could reply, Carmelita insisted, "It's very important that you should speak to my father. If you want to save the dolphins, then he is the *most* important person you must speak to!"

Jody stared at Carmelita. What could she mean?

Luisa raised an eyebrow, looking disbelieving. "You think so?"

Carmelita nodded. "Yes! You see, he's the *alcalde* — I don't know the word in English, but he is very, very important in this town. My father is Señor Guillermo Suarez, and he is the man who gave Señor Martinez permission to keep the dolphins on his premises."

Luisa gasped, astonished. "Your father is the mayor?!"

7

Carmelita's home was not far away. As they followed the girl along a path that rose farther up the beach away from the hotel, Jody felt her spirits rise. She had managed to change the mayor's daughter's mind; maybe her mom and Luisa could make the mayor understand how wrong it was to keep wild dolphins imprisoned in a tiny concrete pool.

Behind her, Jody heard her mother talking to Luisa.

"What did the vet say?" Gina asked.

Luisa sighed. "He reported that the three surviving

dolphins were all young, healthy, and strong. Although they're in some distress now, he's sure they'll soon recover. He may be right. Dolphins usually die before their time in captivity, but they could survive for years to come, no matter how miserable they are. Anyway, all that Señor Martinez wanted to know was whether or not they were diseased — if the one who died might have infected the others."

Jody fell back beside Luisa. "Why did the dolphin die?" she asked.

Luisa sighed. "The stress of the capture and the long journey out of water were too much for her," she explained sadly. "She was pregnant — in no state to travel."

Jody's hand flew to her mouth. She stopped walking and stared at Luisa, feeling tears sting her eyes.

And yet, she felt a stubborn surge of determination. There were still three dolphins to be saved: Chico, Chata, and Luna. Jody was more determined than ever that they should not die in captivity.

"Here we are," Carmelita called out. "*Mi casa* — my

house." They had come to a stone wall with an ornate black iron gate set into it. Carmelita opened the gate and beckoned to her guests to follow.

Behind the wall was a lush and beautiful garden full of flowering shrubs and small, glossy-leaved trees. As they approached the house, a tall, well-built man came out of the door.

"There is my papa," Carmelita said as he came toward them, smiling. She quickly introduced them all.

Guillermo Suarez was a very tall, handsome man with a neatly trimmed black moustache and long, graying sideburns. He had the same beautiful, long-lashed brown eyes as his daughter. He shook each of their hands and gazed intently into their faces as he murmured that he was delighted to make their acquaintances.

"You will, of course, stay for lunch?" he asked, raising his eyebrows.

"That is very kind of you," Gina replied.

"Not at all," he said politely. "It is always a pleasure to have company. I only regret that my wife is in Acapulco for the day, visiting her sister, and so cannot join us. Please follow me inside, and we can become better acquainted."

They followed him indoors to a cool, high-ceilinged living room. Almost as soon as they were seated, a woman in a dark uniform appeared carrying a tray of cold soft drinks that she passed around.

Jody gulped at hers gratefully, suddenly realizing how thirsty she was.

Carmelita began to speak earnestly in Spanish, until her father cut her off.

"We must speak in English to be polite to our guests, *querida*," he said gently.

Carmelita made a face in frustration. "It's too hard for me to explain in English," she complained. Then she brightened as an idea struck her. She turned to Jody. "Jody can tell you about the dolphins!"

Jody nearly choked on her drink. She felt herself blush. It was one thing to explain to Carmelita — but another to explain to the mayor! She looked at Luisa.

Luisa smiled and nodded, then launched into her "official" mode. "Señor Suarez, I work for the Whale and Dolphin Protection League," she began. "My organization sent me here to investigate reports that some recently captured wild dolphins were being kept under extremely cruel conditions."

Señor Suarez frowned. "Do you mean the dolphins at The Beach Bar?" he asked, surprised. "Señor Martinez is not a cruel man! Those reports were wrong, as you must have seen for yourself."

"They weren't wrong, Papa!" Carmelita burst out. "Jody explained it to me! It's cruel to keep dolphins

Carmelita tells her papa the truth.

trapped in a tiny pool like that, with loud music all the time. Dolphins are used to living in the ocean. And loud music — it hurts their ears . . . and Señor Martinez, he has put too much chlorine in the water — it is very bad for them!" Carmelita stopped, out of breath.

Señor Suarez gazed at his daughter thoughtfully. "These people have convinced you, *querida*?" he asked.

Carmelita nodded forcefully. "Yes! If you listen to them, they will make you see that the dolphins *must* be set free — or they will die!"

"Well," he said slowly. "Can this be the same girl who was so excited about the dolphins coming to live in her town?"

"Yes," Carmelita said firmly. "I love dolphins, but now that I know they are not happy at The Beach Bar, I don't want them to stay there. They belong in the sea."

Just then, the maid came back into the room. Señor Suarez rose to his feet. "The meal is served," he said. "Please follow me. We will continue this discussion as we eat."

The dining room offered a view of the garden through French windows. Jody sniffed the air. Smells of melted cheese, fried onions and peppers, and fresh corn tortillas made her mouth water. The long table was spread with delicious-looking food: tortillas, enchiladas, tamales, stuffed peppers, and a crisp, fresh salad.

For the next few minutes the only conversation around the table had to do with the food.

Then Carmelita's father raised the subject of the dolphins again. "I can see you have many strong points to make about the welfare of the dolphins," he told his guests. "It sounds as though they would indeed be better off living free in the ocean . . ."

Jody caught her breath with excitement. Was it really going to be this easy to get the dolphins released?

But Señor Suarez's expression turned regretful as he continued. "However . . . although many people these days believe that *no* animals should ever be confined, not in zoos or on farms, many other people do not agree. I have much sympathy with your viewpoint — I am an animal lover myself," he added, flashing a warm smile across the table at Luisa.

Then his smile faded and he shrugged expressively. "But it is not illegal to keep dolphins for display in this country. I know myself that all of Señor Martinez's papers and permits are in order. I think you will have to agree that no laws are being broken at The Beach Bar."

Jody felt her heart sink. All of a sudden, she had lost her appetite.

"I am not sure I do agree that no laws are being broken, Señor Suarez," Luisa replied calmly.

The mayor raised his eyebrows quizzically.

"There are laws against cruelty to animals," she reminded him. "I am not saying that it is *deliberate* cruelty; Señor Martinez simply doesn't know much about dolphins or how to keep them healthy. Their situation, in a tiny pool in the middle of a noisy public bar, is very stressful and dangerous to them. And it will get worse." She paused. "Do you know about his plan to offer bungee jumping?"

"No. What is this?" Senior Suarez asked, surprised.

Luisa explained. "He told me this in his office. He wants to attract more visitors to The Beach Bar during the day, so he'd decided to set up a bungee jump."

Jody was puzzled. "What does that have to do with the dolphins?" she asked.

Luisa turned to her. "The bungee jumpers would be dropped straight down into the dolphin pool," she said flatly.

Jody gasped in horror. "But — the dolphins could get hurt!" she cried.

"Very likely," Luisa agreed, her face grim. "Kicked and bashed by the jumpers . . . and even if they're not damaged physically, think of their fright, having strange people, whooping and screaming, crashing down on their heads all the time!" She paused. "Dolphins in captivity can also suffer from mental illnesses — just like people who are tortured. And even Señor Martinez should be able to see that having bungee jumpers over your head all day would be torture for anyone, man or dolphin!"

"If he doesn't see it, I do," Señor Suarez assured her. He had gone slightly pale as he listened to her description. "Don't worry, he can't set up such a business without permission — and I won't grant that permission. I'll tell him why, too."

"I tried my best to make him understand why his setup was so cruel to dolphins," Luisa said. "But he couldn't — or wouldn't — see it. You know, many people in the dolphin display industry argue that they serve an educational purpose. They say that in the long run it is good for people and for dolphins to learn more about each other. But Señor Martinez isn't educating anyone! Most of the customers in his bar aren't interested in the dolphins except to tease them. And those who are interested, who might be able to learn, go away thinking dolphins are just like toys, playthings for tourists, instead of living, intelligent animals."

She gazed imploringly at Señor Suarez. "Señor Martinez has no *right* to keep dolphins under such cruel conditions. It's wrong. Please, won't you revoke his permit to keep them?"

It was obvious to them all that Señor Martinez had been moved by Luisa's argument.

Carmelita leaped in with a heartfelt plea: "*Por favor, Papa!* Save the poor dolphins!"

But Señor Suarez sighed and shook his head. "This is a very difficult situation," he replied. "As I said before, Jorge Martinez is acting within the law . . ." He paused, stroking his neat moustache. "What we need is a way to persuade Señor Martinez to give up the dolphins voluntarily," he mused. "But he has spent a lot of money to import them. He won't just agree to lose all that money — unless he gets something in exchange . . ."

"Well, buying them back isn't a problem," Gina said.

They turned to her in surprise. Smiling, Gina explained. "Just before we left, Dr. Taylor told me that PetroCo was *very* eager for our mission to be a success. They are willing to buy the dolphins at the current market price, *and* pay for their return to the wild . . . just so long as WDPL makes it quite clear that the rescue was all because of PetroCo, '*the dolphin's friend,*' in their press releases." Gina shook her head, laughing, as she finished.

Jody smiled with relief. But she noticed that Luisa still looked doubtful. "What's wrong?" she asked.

"Nothing, if Señor Martinez will agree to sell," Luisa replied. "But I must warn you, he told me earlier today that he's already had offers of money from other hoteliers who want dolphins. He said he wouldn't consider selling; he loves the dolphins too much, and he is absolutely certain that they will be a big money-grabber in the years to come. He doesn't want to let them go."

Jody groaned.

"Don't worry," Señor Suarez said slowly, still deep in thought. Suddenly, he smiled around the table at everyone. "We must approach this very cautiously, but now that I have heard all the details, I have an idea for how to make it in Señor Martinez's best interest to sell the dolphins — and make PetroCo — and all of you! — happy."

8

Señor Suarez made them wait until lunch was finished before he would explain his plan.

When the uniformed maid brought in the dessert —
a lusciously creamy-looking flan with a caramelized
sugar topping, the sight of which made Luisa and
Carmelita both sigh with pleasure — he had a quiet
word with her.

A few minutes later, the maid returned with a tray
bearing a silver coffeepot and cups and also a pad of
writing paper and a pen.

Señor Suarez handed the pad and pen to Luisa, who looked at him with surprise.

"Please, finish your dessert first," he urged her. "And then, as we are having our coffee, perhaps you could give some thought to how you would suggest Señor Martinez could restructure The Beach Bar so that his dolphins are assured of a humane and comfortable life."

Luisa's shoulders sagged, but she forced herself to smile. "Well, if you don't think there's any way we could get him to agree to sell," she began unhappily.

"We are working toward that," he told her. "But if he should be stubborn, we must consider the well-being of the dolphins. Just write some ways he could improve their situation."

She nodded and sighed as she picked up the pen. "I could list a lot of improvements, starting with small things," she replied. "But the major changes I'd really like to see would be very expensive . . ."

"That's good," Señor Suarez said quickly.

Luisa and Jody both looked at him in surprise.

He smiled. "In fact, the more expensive the better. Let your imagination run wild — if the dolphins can't have freedom, give them the next best thing."

Luisa looked puzzled. "But surely Señor Martinez won't agree. . . ?" She broke off, staring at Señor Suarez. "Just what *is* your plan, Señor?"

"Please tell us, Papa!" Carmelita cried impatiently.

Her father held up his hands in surrender. "Okay, okay. Here it is . . ." He took a deep breath and settled back in his chair. "Tomorrow morning, Señorita Suarez, you and I will go to The Beach Bar. I will explain to Señor Martinez — who is a man very concerned with pleasing his customers — that I have heard on good authority that no American tourist would stay in a hotel that kept dolphins under such conditions. In fact, rather than making Señor Martinez money, the dolphins might bring his hotel — and our entire town — into disrepute! Therefore, I must insist that he take immediate measures to improve their living conditions."

Señor Suarez smiled and took a sip of coffee. "When he sees how expensive these changes are, I know that Señor Martinez will be a very unhappy man. He may even suggest that he cannot afford them, and will have to sell the dolphins."

"And PetroCo could buy them!" Jody blurted out excitedly.

Señor Suarez nodded.

"But what if Señor Martinez decides to sell the dolphins elsewhere?" Luisa put in worriedly. "He's already told me he's had offers from other hoteliers. The dolphins might end up somewhere even worse!"

"I think he will want to sell to PetroCo," Señor Suarez replied confidently. "You see, I know something else about Señor Martinez," he explained. "You may have guessed that he is a businessman with many interests, always looking for new ventures to make money."

Thinking of the dolphins, and the terrible bungee jump idea, Jody nodded.

Señor Suarez continued. "For the past six months Señor Martinez has been trying to open a vehicle service station on the highway very near to his hotel. He has approached several oil companies, but so far, none of them have agreed to supply him with fuel to sell at a good enough price. Now, if Señor Martinez gives

PetroCo a reason to be grateful to him — by selling, or perhaps even *giving* them the dolphins — wouldn't you think that PetroCo might do something nice for him in return?" He turned his gaze on Gina, raising his eyebrows quizzically.

Gina broke into a broad smile. "Yes, I'll bet they would," she agreed.

Señor Suarez smiled back at her. "I think that Señor Martinez would be willing to bet on that, too," he said.

Carmelita squeezed Jody's arm and leaned over to whisper in her ear. "See? I told you my papa would help!"

In the morning, the mayor arrived to pick up Luisa, Gina, and Jody in an official chauffeur-driven limousine. Carmelita had begged to go, too, Señor Suarez told them. But he'd insisted she must go to school.

Señor Suarez had requested a meeting with Señor Martinez. The hotel owner looked very surprised that Señor Suarez had brought company — and even more surprised when the mayor requested that their meeting should take place in The Beach Bar instead of the hotel's comfortable executive conference room.

For what must have been the first time in The Beach Bar's history, the loud, recorded music was switched off at the owner's command.

While Señor Suarez, Señor Martinez, and Luisa had their discussion in Spanish, Jody went over to the pool with her mother.

She was pleased to find that the overpowering smell of chlorine wasn't so bad this morning, and — maybe in honor of the mayor's visit — the pool seemed to have been properly cleaned.

Chata, Luna, and Chico seemed livelier than they had the day before. When Jody sat down at the edge of the pool, the two females swam right over and poked their heads up into the air to have a look at her.

Jody grinned at them. "Hi, remember me?" she asked.

Luna gaped her mouth several times before sinking below the surface. Chata watched Jody a moment longer, then followed her friend.

Jody looked to see what Chico was up to and saw

that he was swimming very rapidly around the pool. She smiled. He was such a beautiful, sleek, strong animal, and it was good to see him exercising. But very quickly her smile faded as she realized there was something wrong. He was swimming around and around in a mindless, driven way — almost, she thought, as if he was deliberately trying to make himself dizzy. Did dolphins do that? she wondered uneasily.

Jody looked at her mother. Gina looked worried,

Chata and Luna say hello!

too. She winced, and when Jody looked back at the pool to see why, she saw Chico was bumping against the side of the pool. A moment later, he did it again, this time scraping his side along the rough concrete.

Jody caught her breath in sympathy. That had to be painful! Then he did it again.

She stared, not understanding. Dolphins *never* bumped into solid, stationary objects. They had a special sense that allowed them to navigate in total darkness, "hearing" the position of objects to be avoided, like bats. "There's something wrong!" she said anxiously.

"Yes," Gina agreed, putting her arm around Jody. "He knows he's trapped — and he hates it. I hope we can get him out of there before he does himself serious damage."

As they watched, Chico bashed against the rough concrete wall of the pool again. "You mean he's doing that on purpose?" Jody asked in horror.

Gina sighed. "That's my guess."

"But why?" Jody asked.

Her mother shook her head. "Fear, frustration . . .

some animals simply can't adapt to life in captivity," she finished quietly.

Jody felt like crying. She clenched her fists at her sides. They had to save Chico and the other two dolphins — they just had to!

Behind her, the conversation between the hotel owner and the mayor had grown more heated. Señor Martinez shouted angrily. Then Luisa's voice, very calm and friendly, cut into his protests. Amid the Spanish, one word stood out for Jody: "PetroCo."

It seemed to have a magical effect on Señor Martinez. "PetroCo?" he repeated, sounding stunned.

Jody turned around to watch.

Luisa nodded. "PetroCo . . ." Jody couldn't follow her rapid Spanish after that, although she did manage to pick out "*delfines*," the word for dolphins, repeated several times.

Señor Martinez gazed at Luisa as if she had just revealed herself to be his fairy godmother. His dark eyes sparkled. He interrupted her with a stream of passionate language, pointing to himself, then to the dolphin pool. Then he mimed gathering the dolphins into his arms and presenting them, with a low bow, to Luisa.

Noticing that Gina and Jody were staring at him, he switched into English. "Please tell PetroCo that I am most pleased to learn that they are the friend of the dolphins. And assure them that I, Jorge Martinez, am most certainly a friend to PetroCo. They can have my dolphins, with my greatest respect and good wishes, as a gesture of friendship, and the beginning of a long and happy business association."

September 24 — morning, in the air between Acapulco and Kingston.

Mom and I are on our way back to rejoin Dolphin Dreamer. Luisa is staying in Mexico to organize the safe transfer of the dolphins by air. Mom promised that we will stick around beside Amigo del Mar until she gets back, which means we will be on hand to see Chico, Chata, and Luna return to their home waters! I can't wait!

I was kind of worried about the thoughts of them being flown home. It was such a stressful experience for them

119

last time. What if another one died? Wouldn't it be better if they went by sea? But Luisa explained that this time she will be with them to ensure that the International Air Transport Association rules (think I got that right!) were followed to the letter. This means that Luisa and a trained vet will be with them to make sure their skin is kept wet and they don't get too hot or uncomfortable. Unlike last time, when they were just piled onto a mat, they'll be carefully suspended in padded canvas stretchers with slits cut out for their flippers, but they'll also be kept near enough together so they can comfort each other instead of feeling totally alone. The flight won't carry any other passengers or cargo, and it will be especially sound-proofed to cut down on the engine noise. And the flight will be SO much quicker than a sea voyage so that they won't have to be out of water for long.

I am so relieved and happy! What luck that I met Car-melita! She is delighted, too — and very proud of her papa!

At home again, on board *Dolphin Dreamer* in time for dinner, Gina and Jody took turns filling in everybody else about their adventures in Mexico.

"Wow," Craig said wistfully. "Great stuff! Wish I could have been there, to see the three musketeers in action!"

"Four, with Señor Suarez," Gina corrected. "Nothing would have happened without his help!"

"Five, counting Carmelita," Jody said. "We couldn't have met her dad without her!"

Craig sighed. "Well, you didn't miss anything here. It's been pretty quiet."

"Really? You haven't had to chase off gangs of dolphin kidnappers?" Gina teased him.

Craig shook his head, his mouth drooping mournfully. "Nope. Nothing has happened. Nothing at all."

"Oh, come now, I wouldn't say that," Dr. Taylor objected. Pushing aside his empty plate, he peered over his glasses at Craig. "I have managed to get a great deal of work done. In fact, I think I can promise to have the results of the population study ready by dinnertime tomorrow!"

"That's wonderful," Gina said warmly. "I'm sure Luisa will be pleased."

"I've got news, too," Sean announced. He smiled

121

proudly when they all looked at him, and said, "I know my five times table!"

"Yes, he certainly does," Maddie confirmed when Gina looked at her.

Brittany rolled her eyes. "And so would anybody who said it two million times," she muttered.

"Well done," Gina told Sean with a smile. She looked at Jimmy. "How about you, son?"

Jimmy scowled. "Almost," he mumbled.

"You do not," Sean said.

"I said *almost*," Jimmy argued. "I have almost learned it!"

"You just need a little more practice," Maddie said quickly, staving off a quarrel. "We'll do some more work on times tables tomorrow."

"And don't forget our Spanish test," Brittany suddenly said to Maddie. She shot a challenging smile at Jody and said, "After all, I'm sure Jody must have gotten *lots* of practice while she was in Mexico!"

Jody felt her heart sink at the prospect. She couldn't decide whether the grammar or the vocabulary was the hardest part. And with Carmelita and her father, and everyone else they met speaking English so well, she'd hardly had to use her minimal Spanish. Trying to raise her own spirit, she told Maddie, "Luisa said my accent is really improving."

"I'm glad to hear it," Maddie replied. "But there's more to a language than pronunciation. I know you were busy while you were away, so you'd better spend an hour this evening learning some more words," she finished firmly.

Jody sighed and nodded. Back to real life: sniping from Brittany, schoolwork, and tests, she thought. Oh, well, she decided grudgingly, it was fair enough, considering she'd been excused all schoolwork for the past few days. "I'll get started on it now," she promised, as she left the table.

The next morning, before breakfast, Jody was out on deck looking for Frida. She had seen no sign of her the day before. She knew that Luisa would be worried about the solitary bottle-nosed/spotted hybrid and hoped Frida hadn't disappeared.

The sound of a splash made her look over at *Amigo*

del Mar. A dolphin was just plunging back into the water. Jody waited and saw the dolphin leap up again. It was definitely Frida; she got a good look at her scarred, spotted belly when the dolphin arced high into the air beside the WDPL boat.

Frida gave another leap, and then another, moving gradually around the boat. Jody thought it seemed as if the dolphin was trying to get a look at the deck, to check if anyone was on board.

Of course, she thought. Frida must be puzzled — Luisa had never left the boat unoccupied before!

Impulsively, she leaned over the side and called out to Frida, "Luisa's not there! There's nobody there! It's just us, over here!"

As if she'd heard, the dolphin gave a sudden, twisting leap and abandoned *Amigo del Mar* to come racing to the side of *Dolphin Dreamer.*

Then she surged up out of the water, pushing her body high into the air, right in front of Jody. For a brief moment, girl and dolphin were eye-to-eye. Then Frida fell heavily back into the water. Wiping the salt spray off her face, Jody leaned over the side, eager to keep eye contact with the solitary dolphin.

Her pulse was racing. She felt such a strong, strange sense of connection with this wild creature. She was sure that Frida felt it, too. Moving restlessly about in the water, always watching the girl with her bright, intelligent eyes, the dolphin chattered and whistled. She sounded very excited, and she was making more noise than Jody had ever heard from her.

Jody tried with all her might to understand, but her efforts could not turn the sounds into a language she could decipher. And yet, she felt that she knew what Frida was trying to ask her. She hoped she could answer her question.

"Luisa's not here," Jody told the dolphin. "But she's okay. Don't worry! Stick around — she'll be back soon — and so will the other dolphins that belong here, I promise!"

For a long moment, the dolphin was still and silent. Had she understood? Or was Jody wrong about the reason for her distress? Maybe the dolphin was trying to tell her something else. Jody wished that Luisa was there. She'd be able to interpret Frida's behavior much better than she could.

"Luisa will be back soon," Jody called out, gazing intently at the silent, waiting dolphin. "It's okay!"

Frida began to make a rapid clicking sound, interrupted by occasional pops and whistles. She sounded even more agitated now.

Jody chewed her lip, wondering what was wrong. But she could think of nothing more to say or do. She could only watch, uneasily, as Frida plunged beneath the water and headed back toward *Amigo del Mar.*

As Jody watched, Frida swam twice more around Luisa's boat, whistling and clicking loudly before heading out to sea, where she rapidly vanished from sight.

9

September 25 — afternoon, anchored near Jamaica.

I really blew the Spanish test. I don't know why I can't seem to keep the words in my head . . . What makes it worse is that Brittany got 100 percent! Of course, it was a spoken test — with her dyslexia, anything written is much harder for her, but . . . does she have to act so superior about it? Maddie gave me lots more work because she says I need to try harder . . .

Well, I do try! But I find it so difficult. Back at home, Lindsay was better than me at Spanish, so she always helped me. If only I had Lindsay here, instead of Brittany.

"Oh, are you doing your extra Spanish homework in your diary now?"

Brittany's mocking voice interrupted Jody's train of thought. She looked up from her diary, scowling and feeling herself blush.

"You know, Jody, you could do better if you studied a little more instead of always scribbling away in that silly diary," Brittany said pompously.

Jody felt ready to bite Brittany's head off. She tried to think of the most hurtful thing she could say . . . and then suddenly had a better idea. "You're right," she said. "But you're so good at Spanish, Brittany. I don't know how you do it. Will you help me?"

Brittany blinked. It was obvious that this response was the last thing she had expected! For a moment, she was speechless.

"It's so easy for you," Jody pressed.

After a moment Brittany nodded uncertainly. "Well, okay, I guess I could . . ." she began slowly.

"Great!" said Jody. She picked up the list of words that Maddie had given her to study and thrust it at Brittany. "Read those out to me, please," she said.

Brittany's face clouded over at once. She glared angrily at Jody. "I don't want to do it like that," she said, refusing to take the paper.

"Oh, I'm sorry," Jody said, widening her eyes as if she'd forgotten. "You're so good at speaking and remembering. But reading and writing aren't all that easy for you, is it?"

Scowling, Brittany shook her head.

Jody saw she had made her point. She didn't push it any further. She hoped Brittany would agree to a truce now. She watched Brittany thinking about what she had said. "My best friend Lindsay back at home always used to help me with my Spanish homework, and I'd help her with art and music. Kind of a trade . . ." she added quietly.

Gradually, the scowl cleared from Brittany's face. At last, she nodded. "I think I know a way we could work together," she said slowly. "You read me the words, and I'll say them back to you — then you can hear if you're saying them right — and then I'll put the word into a sentence, and you repeat it, and tell me what it means."

Jody smiled and nodded eagerly. "Okay, let's try it!

*   *   *

After half an hour working on Spanish together in their cabin, Jody and Brittany decided it was time to take a break and get some fresh air. Jody could hardly believe they were working together. She hadn't really believed that Brittany would buy her idea!

On deck, Harry and Mei Lin were playing chess, while Cam strolled around restlessly, shining every visible piece of metal, even though they all gleamed from his repeated polishing.

Jody saw her dad standing by the side gazing out to sea, and she went to join him. "Have you seen Frida?" she asked.

"Not recently," he replied. "But there's a reasonably large group of bottle-nosed out there. They're very active; I think they're chasing a shoal of fish."

"Where?" Jody asked excitedly, leaning out to look.

Craig pointed, then took the binoculars from around his neck and handed them to her. "Try these," he suggested. "Once you've had a good look they're easier to spot. They seem to be headed this way."

Jody took the binoculars from her dad. It took her a minute to get them focused. Then, as she scanned the empty, gray-green waves in the direction her father had pointed, she spotted a seagull swooping low. She watched as the gull caught a leaping fish. There seemed to be a lot of fish jumping into the air around there . . . and then she saw a much larger, sleek, gray shape following after the fish . . . and another . . . "Found 'em!" she cried triumphantly.

They were bottle-nosed, all right; strong, healthy and active animals racing through the open sea, occasionally disappearing entirely below the water, then emerging in a graceful leap above the waves. It made such a stark contrast to the three captive dolphins huddled miserably in that dirty pool in Mexico that it brought a lump to Jody's throat.

But the captives would be back here soon, she reminded herself. They, too, would soon be chasing fish and leaping high in the air in what seemed to be expressions of sheer delight in their freedom. They might even be members of this very group, who would welcome them home, she thought.

It did seem to be a large group, the largest they had spotted since their arrival in the waters between Cuba and Jamaica. Already Jody had counted sixteen, and she was sure there were more.

As she turned to scan farther across the water, she caught sight of a boat. It seemed to be following the dolphins. She lowered the binoculars and gazed out at it, frowning. "Did you notice that boat?" she asked her father.

"Looks like a fishing boat," Craig commented. Then he frowned, too. "Although, if they've been fishing, I'm surprised they're not being mobbed by gulls." He turned back to Jody. "Could I have the binocs?"

She handed him the glasses, feeling her heart pounding. She was getting a bad feeling about this boat . . .

Noticing their interest, Cam came closer. "What is it?" he asked curiously.

Craig focused the binoculars on the boat. "Cuban registration," he announced. "Name *El Tiburon*. Definitely a working vessel. Looks like a commercial fishing boat — I can see the nets — but they're certainly not fishing now, and they don't seem to have caught anything recently . . ."

"*El Tiburon* means 'the shark,'" Brittany commented.

132

Jody caught her breath. Sharks were the enemies of dolphins and would attack them. What better name for a boat used to capture dolphins?

"Well, it's just a name," Craig replied.

"It's not a friendly name," Jody said stubbornly. "And it *is* following the dolphins."

"Yes, it is," he agreed. "And those nets . . . they could be used for something other than fish. They could be for catching dolphins. I must admit, if that was a fishing boat, I'd expect to see it fishing. We can see from here that they're practically on top of a big shoal of fish . . ."

Jody groaned with worry and frustration. "They're here to capture dolphins — I just know it!"

"Why don't we follow them?" Cam suggested suddenly.

Jody looked at her father, wanting him to agree.

After a second, Craig nodded. He turned and called Harry away from his chess game. "What are our chances of catching up to those guys if we cast off now, Harry?" he asked. "I'd just like to keep the boat in sight, so we can find out what they're up to."

The captain assessed the situation quickly. His blue

eyes gleamed at the prospect of action. "With the wind in this direction, even if they pick up speed, we shouldn't have any trouble."

"Let's go then," Craig decided.

Harry and Cam quickly got to work.

"Will we be able to stop them if they do start trying to catch dolphins?" Jody asked her father anxiously.

Craig shrugged. "I don't know, sweetheart. But I'm sure it's worth keeping an eye on them. I'm making a note of their registration number," he added, pulling a small notebook and pen from his pocket.

"Are we going to report them to someone?" she asked hopefully.

"We might," Craig said. "It depends . . . I'm hoping that there's a reason why they haven't done anything yet. Maybe they don't have a permit, and they're holding off because they don't want us to witness them doing something illegal. If that is the case, then we'll be able to protect the dolphins just by keeping them in sight. But if they've got a permit . . ." He shook his head and sighed. "Why don't you go below and tell your mother what's happening?"

*   *   *

A mood of excitement overtook them all once they were on the move again.

Harry had been right, and the sleek sailing yacht quickly gained on *El Tiburon*. The winds were strong, and the only problem was keeping from actually overtaking the other boat.

"They're keeping their speed down deliberately," Craig said thoughtfully. "They are definitely following the dolphins, but they don't seem to want to actually catch up to them. They seem content just to observe."

"I wonder why?" said Gina. "I wish there was some way of finding out more."

"Maybe there is," Cam spoke up as he adjusted the set of the mainsail. "Radio," he said simply. "Why not make contact — introduce yourselves, and ask who they are and what their business is."

"They might not tell us the truth," Jody pointed out.

"They sure won't tell us the truth if they're baddies!" Jimmy piped up.

Craig laughed. "They might not tell *us* the truth, but . . . Cam, that was a brilliant suggestion! Instead of making radio contact, we'll just listen in . . . see if we can pick up any transmissions from them to their friends."

"I'll go below," Gina volunteered. "Craig, honey, you keep watching." She turned to Maddie. "Just in case my Spanish isn't up to scratch, would you mind helping me?" she asked.

Jody felt torn. She really didn't want to leave the deck, but she was curious about what they might hear on the radio. She didn't want to miss out on anything!

A few minutes passed, and they continued to sail after *El Tiburon* in the wake of the bottle-nosed dolphins.

Brittany nudged Jody. "This is too boring," she said. "I'm going below, to see if they've heard anything on the radio."

"I'm coming with you," Jody decided.

As they entered the small control room, Jody could hear something that sounded like a weather report in Spanish. "Hear anything interesting?" she asked hopefully.

"Sure," said Maddie, deadpan. "Coast Guard, merchant marine, sailors from three different nations, Spanish-speaking fisherman . . ."

Gina had been fiddling with the dial as Maddie spoke. Maddie suddenly caught her breath and stopped. "Listen!" she hissed.

The signal was loud and clear. A man was speaking in Spanish. Jody caught one word, repeated several times, which she recognized: *delfínes*. She knew that meant "dolphins." Another man replied, also in Spanish. He, too, mentioned *delfínes*. "What are they saying?" she asked, desperate to understand.

Maddie put a finger to her lips. Both she and Gina were listening intently.

Jody chewed her lip with frustration.

Then Brittany leaned close and whispered in her ear, "He says,'We could scoop up as many as we want now. The dolphins are gathered around like ripe fruit. They don't even try to get away. We will never get a better chance!'"

Jody gasped in horror. "They can't!"

Her mother shushed her, pointing to the radio.

Another voice crackled through in reply.

Brittany continued the translation in a low voice. "He says, 'Don't do it. Don't make trouble for me, César or I'll . . .'" Brittany paused, grimacing, then brightened. "'I'll make sure you never work again . . . Why did you have to go out today, anyway, when I told you I don't have any capture permits?'"

They didn't have capture permits! Jody felt more hopeful now.

"César says, 'Rubio, you promised you would get us the permits!'" Brittany went on. "Rubio says, 'I will, I promise, there's no problem. It's all settled except for the stamping. That will happen on Friday, I swear. Just be patient. Dolphins have regular habits, my friend. They will return to the same feeding grounds, at the same time of day, the way that you and your friends go to the same bar every day after work. All you have to do is mark the spot. Then *El Tiburon* can return when we have the official capture permits at the end of the week, and round up as many fine, strong dolphins as we want.'"

There was a pause. Jody held her breath. Then César spoke again.

Brittany puts her Spanish to good use.

Brittany translated: "'Okay. We'll leave the dolphins alone for now, and return later . . .'"

Suddenly there was silence, as the two men signed off.

"Well . . ." said Gina. "At least we've got a few days to think about how to stop them. Come on, let's go tell the others."

On deck, Jody stayed glued to the side with her

brothers and Brittany, watching to see what the men on board *El Tiburon* would do next.

After a few minutes, a man came out of the cabin holding a fluorescent orange ball. Jody watched in bafflement as he threw it over the side. Surely he wasn't trying to play a game with the dolphins?

"It's a fishing float," Cam explained. "It's got a weight on it to keep it more or less in place. They'll just look for it when they want to come back."

"So that's how they're marking the spot," Jody said.

Sure enough, as soon as they'd dropped the marker, the three men vanished from the deck. A moment later, with a throaty engine roar, *El Tiburon* picked up speed and began to move away from the dolphins, chugging back toward the Cuban shore.

10

As soon as the capture boat was out of sight, *Dolphin Dreamer* sailed toward the bright orange fishing float.

Harry managed to steer the boat very close to the float, and Cam leaned out over the side and hauled it on board.

Jody gave a small cheer. Jimmy and Sean punched the air gleefully.

"Now just let 'em try to find their way back here," Sean crowed. "They'll never find the dolphins now!"

"If only it were that simple," their father sighed.

"It may take them a little longer, but they'll find the dolphins," Gina agreed. She looked at the fishing float, dripping onto the deck, and frowned. "Does this count as stealing?" she wondered.

"Nah," Cam said, shaking his head vigorously. "We're not going to *keep* it — we'll just drop it off in another part of the ocean. They'll get it back, eventually. After all, you really can't expect to drop something in the sea and find it again that easily!"

"I don't care if it *is* stealing," Jody said fiercely. "They want to kidnap the dolphins — and that's wrong! I'd help steal their boat to stop them — if I could!" Her mother put an arm around her and gave her a hug.

Gina nodded wearily. She didn't look hopeful. "We'll tell Luisa what we've learned when she makes contact tonight. Maybe she'll know of something we can do," she said.

September 25 — evening, anchored alongside Amigo del Mar.
I'm on deck, writing this in the last light of the day. Frida

has been to visit — still, I'm sure, looking for Luisa. I talked to her for a long time, telling her about El Tiburon and warning her to stay away from them and other boats. I wish I could know that she understood.

Dolphins are so curious and trusting. When they meet people, they seem to have an instinct to try to make friends. Even a few bad experiences don't seem to turn them nasty. That's what people like about them . . . and it's what makes it so easy for people to capture and mistreat them.

Oh, it's so unfair!

"Jody, time for dinner!" Her mother's voice carried clearly to her in the soft, still evening air.

"Coming!" Jody replied. Closing her diary, she took one last look over the side. But if Frida was still around, she was invisible in the gathering darkness.

Everyone else was already at the table, settling down to plates of pasta. The mood was subdued, Jody noticed, with one exception.

Dr. Taylor looked very cheerful. Jody thought it was

probably because he always enjoyed a good meal, until he cleared his throat and said, "I have something to say that will interest you all."

When they all looked at him, he said, "I've finished my work on the data Luisa gave me. I've got the results of the population study."

"Well done," Craig said. "Can you tell us, is it good news or bad news?"

"Ah, well, that depends on how you look at it," Dr. Taylor replied. Carefully laying down his fork, he went on. "It can be clearly demonstrated that the high level of dolphin capture in these waters has had a definite impact. The bottle-nosed population is shrinking rather than remaining stable, as it should."

Jody gasped. "Do you mean they're dying out?" she demanded.

To her relief, Dr. Taylor shook his head. "Oh, no, no! By no means. It's not as grim a picture as that!" He paused to take a sip of iced tea, then went on. "But the numbers of bottle-nosed are indeed lower than the optimum level for a healthy, sustainable population. Therefore . . ." He paused again to sip from his tea.

No one else made a sound. They'd all stopped eating, and everyone was hanging on his words.

Dr. Taylor smiled around the table. "Therefore," he repeated, "the local population cannot sustain further captures. Under international law, further captures in this area should be illegal. And if I know PetroCo, they'll make sure the whole *world* knows the news by tomorrow morning!"

"So, no more capture permits for this area," Gina said, breaking into a smile.

Jody yelled with excitement as she understood. "They're safe! The dolphins are safe . . . you've saved them, Dr. Taylor!"

Dr. Taylor blushed with pleasure. "Oh, please, I wouldn't go so far . . . I can hardly claim that . . ."

The others jumped in with congratulations to assure him that he really had. If Luisa had been there, Jody thought, she probably would have grabbed the dusty old scientist and kissed him soundly on both cheeks! But no one else felt inclined to go quite so far . . .

September 25 — late — so late, it could be the 26th already. Well, Mom and Dad wrote up some press releases and put them out on the Internet. Now that the information is out there, there can be no excuses for any more capture permits being given around here.

Dr. Taylor turned out to be useful after all! I feel like I should be extra nice to him, to make up for all the bad thoughts I've had about him in the past. Luisa was thrilled when we called to give her the news, and she asked to speak to Dr. Taylor. Whatever she said to him made him go bright red! I'm sure if she'd been here, and could have kissed him, he'd have fainted!

Luisa had some good news for us, too. She'll be back — with Chica, Chata, and Luna, who are all still in good health — in three days! Can't wait!

A few days later, Jody stood beside her mother on the forward deck of *Dolphin Dreamer* as they sailed out to welcome the returning dolphins.

Luisa had traveled with the dolphins by air to Kingston. At the airport there, a specialist crew had carefully loaded the dolphins into a container van. They'd been taken to the port and transferred to a boat called *Beluga*, which was owned by the Whale and Dolphin Protection League and used for rescue missions like this. It was Luisa's job to continue to monitor their condition throughout the whole journey.

Once they put out to sea, Luisa had made radio contact with *Dolphin Dreamer* and given Harry the coordinates of where they would be releasing the dolphins. This would be their rendezvous point. Afterward, Luisa would leave *Beluga* to board *Dolphin Dreamer,* and they would take her back to her own boat.

As they sailed away from their anchorage point beside *Amigo del Mar*, Jody noticed they had company. She clutched her mother's arm. "Look! Frida's coming with us!"

Together, they gazed down at the spotted/bottle-nosed hybrid, admiring her swift, graceful leaping progress through the waves alongside the rapidly moving boat.

"I don't suppose she'll stay with us long," Gina said. "She's never followed us before."

That was true, yet Jody felt today was different. "I did tell her we were going to meet Luisa," she said.

Gina laughed. "Oh, she understood you, did she?"

Jody grinned. "I honestly think she did! Even though I can't speak dolphinese . . . or even Spanish!" She joined in with her mother's laughter, but then explained, "I do think she recognized Luisa's name. And I'm sure she noticed how excited we all were this morning — she's guessed that something's up, and she wants to find out what!"

Sure enough, the solitary dolphin stayed with them as they sailed, and she was still there when *Beluga* came into sight.

Cam and Craig worked quickly to shorten the sails as Harry sailed up close alongside the much bigger vessel.

Soon Harry gave orders to "heave to," and *Dolphin Dreamer* slowed to a halt in the water. "Ahoy, *Beluga*," he called through the megaphone.

Jody caught sight of Luisa, along with some people she didn't know, high up on the other boat's deck.

They all waved to each other. Someone handed Luisa a megaphone, and she spoke into it: "Ahoy, all my friends on *Dolphin Dreamer*! I'll be with you just as soon as these dolphins have been set free!"

Jody hugged herself with excitement. She was glad Harry had managed to get them here so quickly.

The first dolphin appeared. It was hoisted in a sort of box, then gently lowered from the side of the ship, down into the water. Jody held her breath as she watched.

The descent from the boat was slow, but smooth. As soon as it was in the water, someone on board pressed a release button, and the sides of the box fell open.

The dolphin — Jody was sure it was Chico — shot out and streaked away.

Jody felt her eyes sting with happy tears as she gave a cheer along with everyone else.

Chata and Luna were released in the same way. Soon, they could see the dolphins reunited in the water. Jody could hear the familiar whistles and clicks that they made as they "talked" to each other.

"Hey, look to starboard," Craig said suddenly. "Is this a welcoming committee, or what?"

Jody turned and gasped as she caught sight of at least a dozen bottle-nosed dolphins swimming rapidly toward them. Within moments, Chata, Luna, and Chico had been absorbed by the group.

It seemed clear that this was the group the captured dolphins had originally been a part of. They were home. The sounds of their excited vocalizing rose on the air like applause.

They didn't stick around. Perhaps they didn't trust these two boats after their recent experiences, or maybe they just weren't interested in something so boringly still. Whatever the reason, the whole group swam away again just as quickly as they had arrived.

Jody gazed after them, feeling, oddly, both happy and sad. "What about Frida?" she wondered aloud. She saw that the solitary dolphin remained close to the side of their boat.

"I think Frida is waiting to meet someone else," Gina said quietly. "Look."

Jody followed her mother's pointing finger and caught her breath with surprise.

Luisa, in a swimsuit, was perched on the railing of

Luisa — home with Frida at last!

the bigger boat. As they watched, she leaped off the side in a graceful dive.

As Luisa plunged into the water, Frida darted forward to welcome home her dearest friend. The two surfaced and dived again, swimming around and alongside each other in graceful harmony, expressing their delight at being together again.

October 1 — afternoon, the Caribbean.
We said good-bye to Luisa, Frida, and Amigo del Mar and cast off this morning.

About an hour ago, while we were in the middle of a history lesson, Harry called us up on deck.

We rushed up topside, and discovered — dolphins to the left of us — dolphins to the right of us! (Or, being properly nautical I should say, to port and starboard.) Dolphin Dreamer was right in the middle of at least 100 bottle-nosed dolphins! (Dad figures he counted 110, Maddie makes it 103.)

Some of them were bow-riding; the others just seemed happy to race alongside us, leaping high into the air, diving, racing ahead, falling back. They stayed with us for half an hour, and I was on the forward deck the whole time, just as close as I could get to them while we were sailing . . . It was wonderful — like a dream.

Maybe they were just in the mood to play with a boat, any boat . . . but I wonder . . . could Chico, Chata, and Luna have been among them? It's nice to think that it was their way of saying "Thanks!"

You will find lots more about dolphins on these web-sites:

The Whale and Dolphin Conservation Society
www.wdcs.org

International Dolphin Watch
www.idw.org